WHAT THE SILK MERCER'S DAUGHTER SAW

A THEO BRYGHT, RUNNER MYSTERY

JOLIE BEAUMONT

ASTER PRESS

Copyright 2012 Linda Feinberg
Cover Design: Linda Feinberg
Illustration: *Habit Amazone en Drap, Journal des Dames et des Modes*, 1803; Public Domain

ISBN 978-0-9885809-0-9

Published and distributed by:
Aster Press
Kansas-Jerusalem
asterpressbooks@gmail.com

CHAPTER I
THEO BRYGHT TAKES ON A NEW CASE

"HOW WOULD YOU LIKE to go to Chester, Bryght?"

Theo Bryght, Bow Street Runner, was seated comfortably by the fire at one of his favorite London public houses. He had just finished a satisfying dinner and a bumper of mulled wine sat by his side. At such a moment he was at peace, and he had no wish to exchange this snug corner of the world for the bumps and jolts of a long carriage journey down England's rut-filled roads.

When he conveyed those sentiments to his young companion, Lord Lauferby replied, while straightening an imaginary wrinkle in his elaborately folded cravat with his perfectly manicured fingertips, "Well, if it all ends in murder do not say I did not try to warn you."

The Bow Street Runner acknowledged the volley by sitting a little—but only a little—straighter in his chair. "Why should there be a murder in Chester? As I recall, Chester is a prosperous town with several good ale houses and an excellent racecourse."

"You have hit upon the problem exactly."

"Have I? Then it must be that you got foxed at an ale house, lost all your blunt at the racecourse, and now your Chester creditor is threatening to put you in the basket."

"I tell you, Bryght, this is serious. Mad Jack Mytton is threatening to kill whoever killed The Miller of Dee."

Theo Bryght returned his attention to his glass. He wondered if the wine was unusually strong this night, since he had no idea what his companion was talking about.

"Let us start again, Lauferby. From the beginning."

"Somebody killed The Miller of Dee while it was stabled at the Chester racecourse."

"The Miller of Dee was a horse, I take it?"

"Of course. What else should it have been?"

"The fog begins to lift. Pray proceed. Why did someone kill this horse?"

"How should I know? The letter I received says only that the horse has been slain and Mad Jack, who sold the horse to my friend, is on his way to Chester to cut off the head of whoever did the deed."

"Will he do it, do you think?"

"They say Mytton is very fond of his horses."

"Still, he had already sold this one. He might just box the ears of the culprit and let the local magistrate do the rest."

"He might. One can never tell with Mad Jack. But Halsey writes …"

"Halsey?"

"My friend. Mr. William Halsey, younger son of Sir Richard Halsey, Baronet."

"Residence?"

"Stanley Hall, north of Chester. Or perhaps east."

"Even if it is situated west or south, if we were to go to Chester — and I make no promise yet — Stanley Hall sounds more promising than resting our weary heads in a stable. I assume Mr. William Halsey was the new owner of the racehorse?"

"He invested practically everything he had. He was hoping The Miller would make his fortune. His family lost most of their blunt when the River Dee silted up and the port moved to Liverpool."

Theo Bryght sighed. He did not like to think of himself as being a mercenary man, but the life of a Bow Street Runner was not a simple one. If a Runner was to enjoy any of the era's many pleasures his meager wages had to be supplemented by private investigative work. This work paid handsomely since the only ones who could afford to hire a Runner privately were the very rich. Due to this economic reality, it made no sense to accept a poorly paid commission in Chester, even if Lauferby supplied the private carriage and the Halseys supplied the food and lodgings.

"It is not just the loss of his horse, though, that has sent Halsey into a brown study," Lauferby continued, after downing the last of his port. "He was hoping to marry."

"The miller's daughter?"

"No, the daughter of a local silk mercer, if you must know."

"Pretty?"

"There is no one prettier in all of England, if Halsey is to be believed."

The Runner smiled. "I raise my glass to the silk mercer's daughter, the prettiest girl in England."

"You can laugh, Bryght, but how is Halsey supposed to get married without any of the ready in his pocket and no prospects of getting any anytime soon? The girl's father is a very wealthy man, and Halsey cannot even offer the family a title. There is absolutely no chance the mercer will let his daughter marry an impoverished younger son."

Theo Bryght lowered his glass. He had no smart answer to that. He himself was an impoverished younger son, having been disinherited, in his younger days, by his father, the fifth Earl of Warrington. He had not regretted losing the respectable living that would have been his, had he agreed to become a clergyman, until recently, when his chosen career as a Bow Street Runner had led him to become involved in solving the mysterious death of Viscount Percy Ainsford Foster Ashe. The young lord had left behind a remarkably pretty widow, Lady Charlotte Ashe, who had managed to disturb the Runner's usually tranquil thoughts with distressing regularity. But what could he offer her? She was a well-to-do "Milady," and he …

"I do not yet see how I can help Mr. Halsey," said the Bow Street Runner, returning his thoughts, which threatened to turn maudlin, to the matter at hand. "Say I do find the horse's killer, the horse would still be dead and Mr. Halsey's money would still be lost."

"Even if you only prevented Mad Jack from murdering the chief suspect, it would be something."

"Why?"

"Well, you see, Halsey writes there is talk, at the racecourse, that the young lady's father, Mr. Thomas Steele, might have had something to do with the crime."

"And so it would not do for Mad Jack to chop off the head of the father of Mr. Halsey's beloved?"

"It would not do at all. Another culprit must be found."

"Perhaps, then, you propose to offer my head as a substitute? If that is your plan, I must tender my regrets. I am rather fond of my head, not the least because it is telling me to stay here, in this comfortable London alehouse, and let a Chester constable sort out the problems of your love-sick friend."

"You disappoint me," said Lord Lauferby, rising unsteadily to his feet. "A gentleman would have seen that Mr. Halsey is nearly in despair and flown to his assistance. If you do not care to help, it can only be because your profession has made you callous. I only pray there will not be another tragedy, and you will not one day have cause to repent your decision." The young lord then left the room with whatever solemn dignity he could muster, after having emptied several bottles of claret at dinner, washed down by a few bottles of port.

Theo Bryght remained in his seat by the fire. He raised his glass to his lips and drank, but the wine had lost much of its sweet warmth. "The Miller of Dee," he mused. "I have heard the name before, somewhere."

A slightly drunken voice suddenly piped up from the table behind him and began to sing:

There was a jolly miller once lived on the river Dee,
He danced and sang from morn till night, no lark so blithe
as he;
And this the burden of his song forever used to be:
'I care for nobody, no not I, if nobody cares for me.
Noooooooooooooo! I care for nobody, if nobody cares for me!'

The Runner reached for his hat and, after bowing slightly in the direction of the tipsy warbler, strode out of the room, shouting, "Lauferby! Get the carriage ready! We leave for Chester tonight!"

CHAPTER II
A HOMECOMING AND A PARTING

"WELL, WE ARE HERE," said the young gentleman, without enthusiasm.

"Yes, we are here," replied the young lady sitting beside him in the carriage.

"It cannot be as dreary as it looks."

The young lady was silent.

While the coachman was busy with supervising the unloading of their trunks, the young gentleman helped his lady descend from the carriage. The two made a striking picture as they stood in the Chester street, for both the young man and the young lady were good looking and smartly dressed, with a hint of foreign climes upon them. But the city's denizens were too wrapped up in their own affairs to notice the pair and give them welcome, and so without further ado they ascended a short but steep staircase that led up to a covered, elevated walkway — part of that Chester anomaly known as "The Rows."

The lady shivered slightly as she gazed down the gallery's dark expanse. "I do not like it here," she whispered.

"It is rather medieval. But we can hardly run back to Italy, Julia, dear. And you do not have to like it here. Just show an interest in the old man's silk business and appreciation for sister Mary's singing and—"

"How do you know Miss Steele sings?"

"If Mary does not sing, then surely Emily is musical. Every English family must have at least one daughter who is musical. Even a silk mercer's family."

"They will not like me."

The young man laughed. "Of course, they will not like you. No one ever likes the bride of the family's heir. She is either too tall or too short. If her hair is dark, they will lament it is not fair. If she is an excellent mistress of her household, they will despise her for her interest in such mundane matters; but woe to the young lady who allows herself to be cheated by the butcher and the baker, especially in a mercantile town like Chester."

"I shall be a guest in this house," said the young lady, smiling for the first time. "The butcher and the baker will be the concern of the Miss Steeles, not mine."

"Sagely said, Mrs. Steele. Your work is to smile and admire, and then smile and admire some more. Leave the rest to me."

The steps they had ascended stood at the end of Bridge Street, where the Bridge Street Row met the Row of Watergate Street, and the young man was unsure which way to turn. Then, as his eyes became accustomed to the gloom, he noticed that a woman was seated in a balcony-like area that overlooked the busy street below.

He could see the woman's face only from profile, since she was seated in front of an easel, upon which stood a canvas. But the profile, with its strong, immobile features seemingly carved from stone, told him much that he needed to know.

The young man, who had been educated in Rome and had received a first-rate education in the art of that city, turned his gaze to the canvas and appraised it with a knowledgeable eye. The brushwork was more than passable he decided, which meant someone had invested in the woman's education. That accorded with his initial impression that this was a woman who not only had a high opinion of her own worth, but expected others to share that opinion, as well. Arranging his speech accordingly, he approached the woman and said, "I beg your pardon, ma'am, but my wife and I are strangers to your charming town. Might you know where I can find the home of Mr. Thomas Steele?"

"You are Mr. Alexander Steele then?"

"You have the advantage of me, ma'am."

"I am your sister, Miss Mary Steele."

The young man experienced a moment of confusion, but not because he did not recognize his own sister. He had been taken away from Chester when he was little more than an infant by the children's mother and had never returned to his native town until this day. Instead, his confusion was caused by a concern that his conversation with his wife had been overheard. Julia, usually so charming and adept in social situations, was also unusually stiff and silent.

Only Mary Steele seemed at her ease, examining the pair with an unabashedly cool and curious eye while she called to a young serving girl, who sprang up from behind the easel as though from the thin air. "Rose, show Mr. and Mrs. Steele to the withdrawing room. And tell Miss Emily our visitors from Italy have arrived."

"Yes, Miss." Rose gave a quick bob and proceeded down the gallery, looking back every few steps to steal a glance at the strangers.

"I shall join you in a few minutes, after I have put away my paints and brushes."

Alexander Steele bowed and then gave his arm to his wife, who, when they had turned away, whispered through the tense smile glued upon her face, "I tell you, I do not like it here."

"Hush," replied the young man. "These Rows have ears."

Miss Emily Steele gave her mirror a worried glance. "Is she dressed very fine?" she asked her lady's maid.

Milly considered the question. Born and bred in Chester, she was hardly a connoisseur of London ladies' fashions, much less the latest fashions on the Continent. Yet one could not work in the home of a silk mercer without learning something about fabric, and so she said with confidence, "Mrs. Steele's frock is very becoming, Miss, but not overly so."

Emily patted down an errant chestnut-colored curl and gave the mirror a last look. She then hurried into the corridor and down the steps. When she reached the drawing room, her natural shyness was vanquished by the emotion of seeing a brother who she had cherished in her heart for her entire young life but had not hoped to meet again.

"Alex!" she called out, as she rushed over to the young man standing by the fireplace. "I am your sister Emily!" She then turned to the dark-haired woman standing beside him and said, "And you must be Alex's wife. I am so happy to meet you. I do hope we shall be friends."

"I hope you will be a sister to her, as well, Emily," said Alexander, "and that you and Mary and I will repair the family circle that was broken by our parents. How is Father, by the way? May I see him?"

"Father usually rests in the afternoon. But after you and Mrs. Steele —"

"Please, call me Julia. Your very kind welcome has made me feel that we have known each other for some time."

"Thank you! And you must call me Emily and tell me all about what it was like to grow up in Italy."

"With the greatest pleasure," said Julia, "and you must tell me all about Chester."

"And before you two women settle down to a nice long chat, Emily, you must tell me about Father. When may I see him?"

"Mary said that first you both must have some refreshments, and then afterward perhaps Mary will let you see him." Noting her brother's quizzical look, Emily continued, "Mary has been in charge of Father, since he became ill."

"Is there no servant who can be trusted with this work?"

"We have hired a woman, but Mary says—"

"I am accustomed to speak for myself, Emily."

Mary Steele stood in the doorway. "I shall ask Mrs. Watson if Father is awake. Mrs. Watson is a very capable nurse, but one cannot expect a hired worker to perform her duties with the same care a member of the family would."

"You are right, of course," said Alexander, "and I am relieved Father's care is under what I am sure is your excellent supervision. He must be very grateful to have such a devoted daughter."

"He does not express gratitude to me, and I do not expect him to do so. We both know what the duties of a daughter are." Mary then turned to Emily and said, "Show Mr. and Mrs. Steele into the dining room. There is a nuncheon buffet laid out on the sideboard."

"You must not mind, Mary," Emily said to the two visitors, after her elder sister had left the room. "If she seems cold and distant, it is because she has taken upon herself so many responsibilities."

"Is Mr. Steele's condition still serious?" asked Julia.

"Yes. We are all so worried. And Mary has had to take over the supervision of the business, in addition to her duties here in the house."

"That is hardly suitable work for a woman," Alexander protested.

"But someone from the family had to do it, and since you ..."

Alexander took his sister's hands and clasped them in his own. "And I was in Italy. But I am here now, Emily. And Julia is here to help, as well. You and Mary will not have to shoulder the burden alone any longer."

After the meal, Julia excused herself and retired to her room to rest. By then Mary had rejoined them, and the three siblings sat alone together for the first time in over twenty years.

"So this is the family home," said Alexander, glancing around the dining room. If the furniture was not remarkable, no expense had been spared when it came to the silver serving pieces. His eye was particularly caught by the silver epergne, laden with fruit, which sat in the center of the table. Crafted in the chinoiserie style, the serving piece's central basket and eight silver side dishes were crowned by a whimsical pagoda-like dome that was topped by a silver pineapple. He wondered who in the family had had the wit and confidence to purchase such a fashionable piece.

"Did our mother never speak of it?" asked Emily.

Alexander gave a start. "I beg your pardon?"

"Did our mother never speak of this house? Did she never describe it to you?"

"No." He then added, "Mother did speak fondly of you both, of course."

"I can understand that you, Alexander, would retain tender feelings for our father's wife," said Mary. "She was, after all, the only parent you have known. But I must ask you to refrain from making any mention of her to our father."

"Does he still hate her?"

"She brought disgrace upon the family."

"Mary, please, must we bring up these things now? Alexander has only just arrived."

"It was you, Emily, who brought up the subject of our mother, who I understand is now mercifully dead."

Alexander bowed his agreement.

"I only wish to warn you, Alexander, so you do not make a fatal blunder."

"*Fatal* blunder? Is that not too strong a word?"

"Our father expressed a desire to see you, before he died," Mary continued, keeping her own intelligent grey eyes on her brother's face. "Do not destroy your chance for reconciliation by attempting to reconcile him with the woman who destroyed his home and happiness by shamefully consorting with another man."

"You speak your mind openly, I see."

"I do so because I want you to understand how things are. Father may be very ill, but he is not so ill that he cannot change his will, should he feel he has good reason to do so."

"That is very kind of you to be so concerned about me," said Alexander.

"I do it not for you," Mary replied. "My one concern is that Father will die in peace, which he can only do if he believes his heir is truly his ..."

"There is no need to finish the sentence. I am aware there was once talk that Mr. Steele was not my true father. It was malicious gossip, of course. But how, may I ask, can I convince my father I am truly his son?"

"You must discover the answer to that yourself."

Rose appeared at the door and dropped her customary hurried curtsy. "Beg your pardon, Miss Steele, but Mrs. Watson says the Master is ready to see Mister Alexander."

"Thank you, Rose," Mary replied.

Emily walked with Alexander to the door. "Good luck," she whispered, before he began the long climb up the stairs.

Thomas Steele's bedroom must look onto a back alleyway, Alexander decided. Otherwise, a Chester home must exist in a perpetual state of twilight. Yet even if the room had been flooded with the brilliant sunlight of a Roman morning, he doubted it would have lifted his sinking emotions. For there was something grimly overwhelming about a life hovering on the margin of death — and he was sure the man lying in the sickbed would soon be embarking on that last horrific journey.

Mrs. Watson, the very picture of plump and rosy good health, beckoned for the young man to come forward. When he too stood by the bed, she called out to the dying man, "Here is your son, Mr. Steele, come all the way from Rome to see you."

The elderly man opened one glassy eye.

"I will leave you two gentlemen now, as I am sure you have much to say to one another." She then said to Alexander, in a lower tone of voice, "If you should need me, I'll be sitting in the corridor."

The woman left and shut the door behind her.

The elderly man continued to stare at the younger one with his one good eye.

"Are you comfortable, Father?"

The old man moved his lips violently, but it was a struggle to no purpose. His most recent stroke had left him half-paralyzed and unable to articulate no more than a few words.

"Shall I give you something to drink ... sir?"

Alexander took up a pitcher that was standing on a side table and poured some of the contents into a glass. His hands shook slightly and some of the liquid spilled onto the table. Removing a handkerchief, he carefully wiped the table clean, and wiped the glass as well. It was then that he heard the sound of a window being raised.

He spun around. For a moment it was hard to determine who was more surprised, the young man or the intruder. But since Alexander was tall and the intruder was short—not to mention under ten years of age—Alexander was the first to regain his composure.

"And who may you be, young man?"

"Sam, sir, from the racecourse."

"And what business, Sam, have you with Mr. Steele? Was there a race meeting today?"

"No, sir, just training. Mr. Steele was used to enjoy a nice piece of gossip from the stables. Said it cheered him up. Said it did him more good than all them drops and broths Doctor and Miss were always pouring down his gullet."

Sam might have continued in this vein for some time, having warmed to his subject, if not for the fact that the door had burst open and the "Miss" in question, Mary Steele, who was armed with a broom, had rushed into the room.

"I thought I heard your voice! Get out the way you came, this instant! I will not have you upsetting Mr. Steele with your foolish talk."

During this diatribe, the stable boy scurried toward the window, but not by the most direct route. To avoid the long arm of the broom, he darted under the bed and jumped over a chair, before leaping onto a side table and heaving himself out the window. Where the boy went from there, Alexander did not know. He watched as Mary Steele slammed the window shut and secured the latch. There would be no more intruders that day, her determined look seemed to say, as she straightened the things on the table and picked up the overturned chair.

She then said to her father, "That boy has let a draft into the room. Would you like a hot water bottle?"

Whether the elderly man said yes or no, Alexander could not say. But Mary seemed to know. She called to Mrs. Watson to have one prepared, and then she said to Alexander, "I think it best if you continue your conversation tomorrow. Father is tired now."

Alexander looked down at the old man, who was still staring at him with his one good eye. He then said to Mary, "I should like just like another minute or two, in private."

"As you wish."

When Mary returned to the corridor she saw that Julia Steele was standing by the door to her room.

"Is anything wrong, Miss Steele?"

"No, Mrs. Steele. Why should there be anything wrong?"

Seeing no further conversation was intended, Julia made a movement to return to her room. Mary, meanwhile, was halfway down the stairs when the front bell rang and a servant hastened to answer the door.

Mr. Tilson, the manager of the Steele silk mercer business, stood in the doorway. He removed his hat from his balding head when he saw Mary Steele, who was descending the remaining steps to greet him.

"I beg your pardon, Miss Steele, for disturbing you, but there are some cheques that must be signed."

"Not at all, Mr. Tilson. Please come with me to the study."

Julia Steele, who had retraced her steps back to the top of the staircase, silently watched the two, until they disappeared down the corridor. She was joined by Emily Steele, who asked, "Who was at the door, Julia?"

"I believe his name was Pilson, or perhaps Tilson."

Emily was visibly disappointed.

"Miss Steele seemed very happy to see him," Julia commented. "Who is he? Her lover?"

Emily blushed. "This is Chester, Julia, not Italy. You must not say things like that here."

Julia laughed. "But is it true? I thought I detected a smile on Miss Steele's face, something I did not see when she greeted her brother."

Emily shook her head. She could not imagine anyone falling in love with Mr. Tilson, who was not only a middle-aged bachelor, but had a distressing tendency to continually suffer from the sniffles, amongst other common ailments.

"Mr. Tilson is the manager of our family's business. I am certain there is nothing improper about his visits."

Julia sighed. Taking Emily's arm and turning back toward their rooms, she said, "You are most probably right, dear Emily. A pity."

It was while they were all dressing for dinner that the alarum — in the form of Rose shrieking at the top of her lungs — was first heard.

"What is it, Rose?" asked Emily, who arrived in the corridor first.

But Rose could only point with a trembling arm to the open door that led into the sick room.

Carefully skirting several pieces of broken china that were the remnants of what had been a light evening meal before Rose dropped the entire tray on the floor, Emily made her way towards the bed.

"What has happened, Emily?" asked Mary, who had also entered the room, her undressed hair still hanging about her neck.

"Oh, Mary," the younger sister said with a sob, "Father is dead."

CHAPTER III
BUBBLE AND SQUEAK

IN THE END, THEO BRYGHT and Lord Lauferby did not lodge at Stanley Hall for more than one night. Their hasty departure was not due to the reception they had received, which had been more than adequate. Their rooms were spacious and well aired, while the serving man appointed to unpack Theo Bryght's trunk had not visibly turned up his nose at the Runner's clothes, whatever his thoughts were in private. Lord Lauferby, who had brought his own manservant, of course, caused his valet no such discomfort.

At the dinner table, Sir Richard was an amiable host, having played the part of county squire for many long and generally complacent years. Eager to hear news from London and willing to instruct his guests about the more interesting points of the surrounding Cheshire neighborhood, he kept the conversation flowing, along with the excellent wine from his cellar, more than making up for the icy reserve of Lady Halsey, who conversed with Lord Lauferby but barely marked the Runner's presence. Indeed, if it had not been for the brooding presence of Sir Richard's son, William — a passably good-looking fellow, the Bow Street Runner decided, although in an entirely conventional way that hinted, at best, at a still unformed character, and at worst at a weakness of resolve — one might have thought Theo Bryght and Lord Lauferby had come to Cheshire for no other reason than to enjoy some outdoor sport in the pleasant country air.

Yet despite the tempting invitation to do some pond fishing — the estate was not sufficiently close to the River

Dee to make river fishing a comfortable possibility —
Theo Bryght reluctantly came to the realization that
Stanley Hall was too far away from Chester to be useful
to his investigation. He therefore expressed a wish to be
lodged at a more central location and the next morning
found him lodged at the Bear and Billet, a Chester inn
located on Lower Bridge Street, near both the River Dee
and the Roodee, Chester's racecourse. There he partook
of a substantial breakfast of toast, eggs and a plate of
bubble and squeak.

He had the pleasure of introducing this last dish, a
homey concoction of leftover meat and cabbage that
"bubbled and squeaked" when fried over the open fire,
to Lord Lauferby, who was accustomed to more genteel
fare. After a hesitant first taste, the younger man
devoured the dish with so much enthusiasm that a
second plate was called for.

While they waited, Lauferby surveyed the inn's
dining room, eyeing with approval the half-timbered roof
and oak paneling. "A veritable relic of old England," he
commented. "I would not be surprised if there is a
priest's hole hiding behind that paneling."

He then walked over to the hearth to examine a
decorative object called a silent companion — a trompe
l'oeil painted figure, which had been popular
conversation pieces during the 1600s. This one was a
painted figure of a servant girl with ruddy cheeks and an
impish smile, carrying on her arm a lifelike painted
basket filled with bread and fruit. She was placed so that
she stood before the hearth, acting as a screen to shield
the diners from the fire.

"I have not seen one of these things since I was a
boy," Lauferby commented. "An old aunt of mine had
one of them, only hers was a solider in armor. She kept it

outside her bedroom door — said it would scare away intruders."

"Did it?" asked Bryght.

"I do not know about intruders, for I cannot think who would have cared to visit her room late at night. But it certainly scared me. I did not dare leave my room until morning."

Their conversation was interrupted by the arrival of the platter heaped with a second portion of bubble and squeak. They were still at table when William Halsey arrived. The young man declined their invitation to join them, explaining he had breakfasted at his home. What he did not say, although it was apparent from his demeanor, was that he was anxious to begin the investigation concerning the death of his horse. Therefore, after a few more mouthfuls, Lord Lauferby bade a reluctant goodbye to his breakfast, and the Runner swallowed the last of his coffee.

When they went into the street, they were greeted by a blast of bone-chilling air. Halsey assured the other two the Roodee was not far. Indeed, by the look on his face it was apparent that in his thoughts, at least, he was already there. He was therefore more than a little surprised when the London Runner expressed a desire to first see the "famous walls of Chester."

"Or so they are described in this most interesting albeit ancient guide I found in my room," said Theo Bryght, pulling out from his great coat's pocket a much-thumbed-through book that was really no more than a pamphlet. "Let Wordsworth enthuse over his lakes, the author of this charming work, Taylor seems to be his name, would have us admire Chester's walls, and admire Chester's walls we shall."

Halsey was about to speak out his dismay, but he recovered his sense of propriety in time to make a civil answer. "As you please, Mr. Bryght. The walls are very fine, and few who see them are disappointed." However, he could not resist adding, "Although I personally feel they can be seen to their best advantage when the sun is setting and it paints the walls with a remarkable reddish hue."

"I do not doubt you are correct, Mr. Halsey. But I believe in seizing the opportunity while I may. And if I am not mistaken, we shall not see much of the sun today. Those storm clouds seem determined to lodge here for a good while."

There was no need for the young man to reply, since the Runner, followed by Lord Lauferby, was already heading down Bridge Street, in the direction of the River Dee. When the trio had climbed up the steps that led to the promenade on top of the wall, Bryght began to enthusiastically read from his guide book, "'Chester is a City pleasantly situated on the River Dee (here he pointed down to the river). It is of a Square forme, surrounded with a Stone wall (here he pointed to the wall), on which there is a walkway quite round the Town, 2 miles in compasse, and kept in very good repaire.'"

Here Bryght stopped his reading and gave a look around.

"The walls are kept in very good repair. Now why is that? I can understand why the Romans bothered with them. They built them. And good, sturdy city walls certainly came in handy when the Saxons were battling it out with the Danes and Normans. But why were the walls never broken down afterward, as happened in other cities in England?"

"Wales is not too far away," Halsey replied. "Then there was all that trouble during the Civil War. Chester was a Royalist town. Charles I watched the defeat of his army from one of the walls' towers, the Phoenix. We will come to it further on. It is a popular spot to visit for ladies and gentlemen taking a walk round the promenade."

"How are the mighty fallen; where cannon balls once flew, the parasol now reigns. And speaking of falling," said the Runner, looking down toward the river, "this weir seems like a delightful place to drown."

"Charming, but we are not here to investigate a drowning," said Lauferby, who sympathized with his friend's desire to not waste time.

"Not yet," Bryght replied cheerfully. "But the day is still young."

Bryght continued to gaze down at the weir, which was turning the calm waters of the River Dee into a dangerous, deafening whirling pool. Beyond the weir, the river regained its serene demeanor and glided placidly below the old Chester Bridge, before continuing on its way to the sea. He wondered if this was an apt metaphor for the person he was seeking. For twenty, thirty, or fifty years the person glided calmly through life. Then one day something happened, something so distressing the person became momentarily crazed and killed the Miller of Dee. When the rage passed, the person returned to his accustomed state of calm. Perhaps at this very moment he was discussing the price of corn or the state of the roads over a friendly glass of ale. Or perhaps the weir was the metaphor, in its totality. Perhaps the person's entire inner life had been lived inside a weir, and the stabbing of the horse was just one of many times this person's inner turmoil had escaped into the light, though he had never yet been apprehended.

Since it was much too early to try to guess which type of person he was looking for, the Runner returned his thoughts to his two companions and asked, "Which way shall we go?"

"If you wish to visit the Cathedral, we should continue left," said Halsey, insisting on playing the role of the polite host, despite his personal feelings.

"And if we were to continue to the right?"

"That way leads to the Castle, and the racecourse; though it looks like the racecourse may be coming to us."

Bryght and Lauferby turned to where Halsey was looking. Running toward them, as though pursued by demons, was a boy.

"What is all this, Sam?" Halsey asked, catching the boy by the back of his shirt as Sam tried to dart past them.

It took the boy several moments until he realized he was among friends, or at least one friend he recognized. But even so, he was determined to escape.

"Let me go, Mr. Halsey. They're after me."

"Who, Sam?"

"The law, sir. But I didn't do it. Will you tell them, sir?"

Theo Bryght said to Halsey, "I suggest we continue this conversation back at the inn, before the law overtakes us."

When they were safely seated in a private sitting room, Sam was given a plate of food and a mug of ale, which he could barely enjoy since every few minutes he turned his head toward the closed door, certain that doom was about to walk through it at any moment. It was only after considerable coaxing — and a threat from

Bryght that he would dub the boy "Bubble and Squeak" if he did not settle down and stop jumping up at every sound — that Sam was able to relax, and even laugh, and relate his tale.

"It was quiet at the stables yesterday," the boy began, "on account of Jim Beane —"

"A jockey," Mr. Halsey explained to the others.

"Jim he was having a sorry case of the wheezes and shivers," Sam continued, "and Young Peter —"

"The trainer," Mr. Halsey again interjected for the benefit of Bryght and Lauferby. "He is really not so young, but there is also an Old Peter, who is a kind of watchman, I suppose. Old Peter has been a fixture at the stables for as long as anyone can remember. He lives there and gives the floor a sweep with his broom once in a while, to earn his keep."

"But even though you are sure he spends most of his time sleeping," said Bryght, "he is the one who knows all that goes on."

"Yes, that describes Old Peter perfectly."

Sam was then asked to continue. "Young Peter was moping about as well, and so Old Peter says to me, 'Sam,' he says, 'there's nothing to be done. Go tell Mr. Steele we'll take his horse for a run tomorrow, if Jim or Young Peter is feeling up to it.'"

"This Mr. Steele —"

"He is a well-known silk mercer here in Chester," Halsey said to the Runner. "He is also the father of the young lady I should like to marry, if she would do me the honor of bestowing upon me her hand."

"So, Sam, you went to Mr. Steele's home. What happened next?" Bryght asked.

Sam chewed on his mutton thoughtfully, before shaking his head. "I can't rightfully say, sir. When I climbed through the back window —"

"Is that your usual means of entry into the house?"

Sam nodded. "Mr. Steele, before he got all funny and forgot how to talk and move his right hand, said to me, 'Sam,' he says, 'women don't understand about racing, so you'd best not come in through the front door. You come in through the bedroom window and we'll have our little talk and no one need be the wiser.' That means no one in the house knew when I come and gone except Mr. Steele and me."

"What did you and Mr. Steele talk about? Did he give you money to place a bet?"

"When the race meeting was on, he did," Sam replied. "Other times, we would just talk. He liked to hear what was going on in the stables. He has a horse there, Cavalier. He was counting on it throwing dirt into the eyes of The Miller of Dee."

Sam then glanced over at Mr. Halsey. But before Mr. Halsey could speak, the Runner asked another question. "There was a rivalry, then, between Mr. Steele and Mr. Halsey?"

"If you mean did they each want their own horse to win, I suppose there was."

Theo Bryght smiled. Put that way, the rivalry between the two men was the most natural thing in the world. But did the animosity go deeper, he wondered?

"Very well, Sam, you are now in Mr. Steele's bedroom, having entered through the window. What happened next?"

"I didn't do it!"

"Do what?"

"Put poison in Mr. Steele's glass!"

For a moment, the Runner was too stunned to speak. Then he asked, "Why should anyone think you did such a thing?"

"Because he's dead."

Now it was the turn of William Halsey to be astonished. "Thomas Steele is dead? When did it happen?"

"How should I know when it happened?" the boy wailed. "He was alive enough when his daughter chased me around the room with her broom."

"Who chased you?" the Runner asked. "Do you know her name?"

"Miss Steele, it was."

"That would be Miss Mary Steele," Halsey explained, "the older sister of the lady I wish to marry."

"Was there anyone else in the room?" asked Bryght.

"There was a gentleman, sir. He was already in the room when I pulled up the window sash. I never saw him before. Could be he was a new doctor. "

"But Mr. Steele was alive, you say? How do you know? Did he speak to you?"

"He couldn't speak to anyone anymore. But he saw me, I know, with his one good eye. And anyways, this was in the afternoon and they says he died right before the family was going to have their dinner. I was back at the stables by then. Old Peter will tell you. You won't let them take me to the Castle, will you, Mr. Halsey?"

"The Castle is where the jail is," Halsey explained to the Runner and Lord Lauferby.

"I still do not understand why they suspect you, Sam," said Theo Bryght. "Did you say all this to the constable?"

"And let 'em string me up without a fight? When I heard the constable was looking for me, I ran."

IT WAS LATER ESTABLISHED that the Chester authorities had no immediate desire to put a noose around Sam's young neck. To the delight of the town's gossips, the magistrate had requested that an inquest be held to examine the "mysterious circumstances" surrounding the death of Mr. Thomas Steele, silk mercer, and Sam had been called to give testimony.

"Just tell the magistrate what you told us," Bryght said to the boy. "Though I suggest you leave out the bit about the broom. Say instead Miss Steele expressed a strong desire that you depart the room at once."

Sam, having been freshly bathed and given a clean suit of clothes, arrived at the inquest in the company of his benefactor, Mr. Halsey. Theo Bryght and Lord Lauferby arrived separately. The Runner had made his presence known to the magistrate, who had given him leave to conduct his inquiries about The Miller of Dee. But since he had not been asked to investigate the death of Thomas Steele, he sat in the gallery, with the rest of the people. From the gallery he could view the proceedings while hidden under the cloak of anonymity, a guise that suited him, for the present. It was only after the inquest had concluded for the day that he regretted his decision not to play a more visible part and take charge of Sam himself.

The magistrate, noting the large crowd squeezed into the room, brought the proceedings to order with suitable aplomb. A constable by the name of Merriweather was called first. While Merriweather made his way to the front of the room, Theo Bryght took in the scene. The bereaved family was not hard to discover. The two ladies dressed in black were most certainly the daughters of the dead man. Beside them sat a young man with a black armband, and Bryght wondered who he was.

Meanwhile, Constable Merriweather had begun to give his account of the facts. In brief, he was summoned to Number 10, Bridge Street Row, home of Mr. Thomas Steele, well-known Chester silk mercer, at approximately six o'clock in the evening. He was admitted into the home by a parlor maid named Margaret (the magistrate made a note of the name), who informed him that Mr. Carlstone, the well-known Chester physician (the magistrate nodded to Mr. Carlstone), was awaiting his presence upstairs.

When he arrived in the sickroom, the constable was much surprised to see the sorry further alteration that had occurred in Mr. Steele's health during the weeks preceding the mercer's death.

"Your meaning, Constable Merriweather?"

"Meaning, sir, Mr. Steele had once been a stocky, bullish sort of man and now he appeared to be no more than a bag of skin and bones."

Proceeding with his tale, the constable described the scene that then confronted his eyes. Mr. Steele, before he died, had apparently suffered some great shock for his limbs were all contorted. But upon his commenting that it seemed Mr. Steele had suffered a bout of apoplexy, the physician had replied, in these words, "Not this time, Constable. I am willing to stake my reputation upon it. Mr. Steele has been poisoned."

At this point in Constable Merriweather's testimony pandemonium broke out in the room. When order was restored, the magistrate decided to interrupt the constable's testimony, for the interim, and ask the physician to stand.

"I received a message to please hurry to Mr. Steele's home," began the physician, "for a terrible tragedy had occurred. Those were the words of the messenger, a young boy by the name of Joe, I believe. As the message had been sent by Miss Steele, whom I knew from experience to be a most level-headed young woman, I proceeded to Bridge Street at once."

"You have attended Mr. Steele for how long, sir?" asked the magistrate.

"I have been the family's physician for more than twenty years."

"You were therefore familiar with the illness that left Mr. Steele bedridden?"

"Oh, yes. Mr. Steele suffered from apoplexy. The first and second attacks were relatively mild ones. But the third attack left him partially paralyzed and affected his speech."

"Yet you do not consider apoplexy to be the cause of Mr. Steele's death?"

"No, I do not."

"Can you tell us why?"

"I observed three curious facts. The first was that the bedclothes showed that Mr. Steele had experienced severe problems of the stomach before he died. Due to the large number of ladies present in the room, I shall not go into detail here."

The magistrate glared vaguely in the direction of the ladies, before asking, "Could that not have been due to his supper not agreeing with him, Mr. Carlstone?"

"Hardly," replied the physician, with a slight smile. "After his third attack, Mr. Steele was unable to digest solid foods. His diet consisted primarily of porridge and broth, neither of which would normally cause such a violent reaction."

"Your second point, sir?"

"A glass had fallen to the floor, beside the bed. The glass was almost empty, but a few drops of the contents remained. I brought one of those drops to my own lips. The acrid taste alerted me immediately to the possibility of poison."

"Possibility, you say? Yet by the time Constable Merriweather arrived, you were certain. What happened to convince you, Mr. Carlstone?"

"Having stooped to retrieve the glass, I was in a position to observe closely Mr. Steele's left hand, which was dangling near the floor. Clasped within his fingers was a small wooden square, the kind children use to learn their letters. On the square was painted the letter P."

"P?"

"P."

The magistrate opened and closed his mouth several times in quick succession. "And from that you surmised Mr. Steele had been poisoned? From a child's alphabet tile?"

"I would not necessarily have reached this conclusion on my own, but the testimony of the hired nurse, Mrs. Watson, convinced me that the deceased, upon realizing that poison had been placed in his glass, attempted to alert ..." Mr. Carlstone paused. While he searched for the correct word, his eyes carefully avoided the bench where the Steele family sat. "He attempted to alert the household and the authorities of that fact."

An ocean of murmurs accompanied Mr. Carlstone to his seat. Mrs. Watson was the next person who was called. The nurse approached the front of the room with great dignity, only stopping to wink and wave at a half dozen of her closest friends.

Yes, she was Chester born and bred, though she had moved away when she married Mr. Watson, only returning to her place of birth after his death (apron to the left eye, the right one apparently devoid of tears). No, she had not always been a nurse. Until Mr. Watson passed away last year, she had always minded her own business in her own house. But Mr. Watson, although a good man in every other respect, had not left her much except the house where they had lived, and a person could not eat the pots and pans, could they? And so she had sold the house, returned to Chester, and hired herself out as a nurse, first to old Mrs. Cranford, who passed away in the early spring, and then to young Mrs. Morecombe, who gave birth to twins, as everyone knows, and needed some help looking after the little darlings. But now, thanks to the good Lord, the happy mother was right as rain and did not need Mrs. Watson to look after her or the babies anymore, which was why Mrs. Watson was happy to oblige Miss Steele when that lady asked Mrs. Watson to help with the nursing of poor Mr. Steele, who was suffering something terrible after his third attack.

"Mr. Steele, then, was in great pain?" asked the magistrate, when he could finally enter a word.

"Not so much pain of the body, sir, but I saw it pained him mightily that he couldn't speak more than a word or two. So one day I said to myself, 'Mrs. Watson, see what is going on in this sickroom. There is Mr. Steele, struggling to tell you something. Here are you, struggling to hear what is. Something must be done to remedy this situation.' And that's when I thought of the box of letters I had saved from my childhood, a gift from my dear mother, who insisted I should learn to read."

"Indeed?" said the magistrate, who did not entirely improve of people acquiring knowledge unnecessary for their station in life.

"She had been widowed young, you see, sir, and cheated of her property when she signed a piece of paper upon the advice of an unscrupulous lawyer, and all because she couldn't read a word. So she said to us, her children, 'My dears, you shall not be swindled like your poor old Mama. You shall learn these letters if your tutor has to beat them into your wooden heads. I give him permission. So get to it and don't let me hear you complaining.'"

Mrs. Watson then explained that she had brought the box of letters to the sickroom, and Mr. Steele had been well pleased to receive them. When he wanted his tea, he could spell out the word "tea" and when he was cold he could spell out the word "cold" and when he wanted to bet on a horse … Here the good woman stopped and the onlookers laughed and the magistrate rapped on the table and called for order.

"When did you last see Mr. Steele alive, Mrs. Watson?"

"He was alive when the gentleman sitting beside Miss Emily Steele came into the sickroom to talk to him."

"You are referring to Mr. Alexander Steele, the son of the deceased?"

Hundreds of heads turned to catch a glimpse of this heretofore unknown person.

"Yes, sir. And he was alive when I brought up a hot water bottle. That would have been after Sam, the stable boy, left the back window open and let in all the cold air."

Sam was about to spring up from his seat and protest, but Mr. Halsey clamped a firm hand upon the boy's shoulder and he slumped back onto his seat.

"And after that?" asked the magistrate.

"After that I closed the curtains and left Mr. Steele to rest. He usually rested in the afternoon. I went down to the kitchen to have my supper, and the next thing I knew Rose was screaming her head off and Miss Emily was sobbing and …"

"In a word, Mr. Steele was dead?"

Mrs. Watson again dabbed at her eye with her apron, by way of reply. She then explained she had wanted to arrange the body so it would rest more comfortably, but Miss Steele told her to leave it as it was, until Mr. Carlstone came. Miss Steele did ask her, though, to pick up the pieces of broken crockery — Rose had dropped the tray that had upon it Mr. Steele's supper — and while Mrs. Watson was doing this she saw that a glass was on the floor by the bedside and she was about to put it on the side table, where it usually sat, when she saw the wooden tile in Mr. Steele's hand.

"I saw he was grasping the letter P," Mrs. Watson continued, "and I wondered what he had wanted to say. The word 'pray' came to my mind, which I think is natural considering the situation, but somehow I never thought of Mr. Steele as being a praying sort of man. Then I thought perhaps he might have had a hankering for some fruit — a peach or a plum or a pear — because the sick they do get a hunger for certain foods, sometimes. It was only when I saw the other letters on the table I realized what poor Mr. Steele was trying to say."

"And what letters were they, Mrs. Watson? Finish your story. We have not got all day."

"There was an O, sir, and an S and I and an N, and me being a God-fearing woman I said to myself, 'The Lord is merciful. Mr. Steele's last thoughts were directed toward Heaven, after all, for here are his last words, for all to see — O, Sin — showing he had repented of whatever wickedness he had done in this world.' And I don't mean any disrespect to Mr. Steele or his family, for we all have reason to fear the Judgment Day, as I'm sure the vicar will agree."

"We will leave out the vicar for now, Mrs. Watson. How did this virtuous thought become something else by the time the physician arrived?"

"It was the P, of course. The letter in Mr. Steele's hand."

The magistrate, whose strong point was not spelling, made up for his confusion by staring haughtily at the witness. "Make your words plain, for the benefit of the jury," he snapped.

"P-O-I-S-N. And although the word is missing an O, since my box has only one tile for each of the letters, there is no doubt in my mind what Mr. Steele meant to say. Poison, sir! Murder, sir! I cannot make my words plainer than that!"

CHAPTER V
THE INQUEST CONTINUES

AFTER MRS. WATSON'S TESTIMONY there was nothing to do but adjourn for an hour, so the scandalized citizens of Chester could discuss the murder over cold meat and ale. Then the inquest resumed and an examination of the family members began.

Miss Emily Steele had very little to say. She had not visited her father during the day — due to her excitement over greeting her brother after so many years — and she was sure she would never forgive herself for neglecting her father on the last day of his life. She had not noticed her dead father holding anything in his left hand. The shock of his death had overwhelmed her.

"Quite so, quite so, my dear," said the magistrate, who still had an eye for a pretty girl, despite his advanced years.

Miss Mary Steele was asked to give testimony next. She had been accustomed to enter her father's room often during the day, to see if he needed anything, and that day had been no different.

"Nothing unusual occurred then?" asked the magistrate.

"I did not say that, sir," replied Miss Steele.

Miss Steele then described the incident with Sam, omitting the broom but describing in great detail the boy's scampering about the room.

"And so someone might have placed the poison in Mr. Steele's glass, during the confusion?" asked the magistrate.

Miss Steele's eyes looked down at her gloved hands and stayed there. Mr. Alexander Steele, upon understanding the meaning of the magistrate's words — for who could this "someone" be if not him? — blushed at the insinuation. And if not for the steadying hand of Mr. Halsey, Sam, always ready to pop up from his seat, would have popped up then and there and screamed out, "I didn't do it!"

The magistrate asked Miss Steele to continue with her testimony. Miss Steele said she had looked in on her father once more during the afternoon. No, she could not remember the time. It had been such a busy day, what with the arrival of her brother and his wife from Italy.

"Did Mr. Steele seem ill, or in distress?"

"No, he appeared to be sleeping peacefully."

"Was that the last time you saw your father alive, Miss Steele?"

"Yes."

"How did you learn of Mr. Steele's death?"

"I heard a crash, the sound of crockery breaking, while I was dressing for dinner. Then I heard Rose, one of our servants, wailing. I rushed out to see what had happened. My sister had reached my father's room before me. It was she who told me Mr. Steele was dead."

"Did you notice that Mr. Steele was holding an alphabet tile in his hand?"

"Not at first. My sister was sobbing, and I feared she might collapse in hysterics. I therefore asked Mrs. Watson, who had by this time also come into the room, to take Miss Emily back to her room and try to calm her down."

"I thought you asked Mrs. Watson to pick up the broken crockery."

"I have not finished with my testimony, sir. I can explain, if you will allow me to proceed."

The magistrate, chastised and not liking it much, waved her onward.

"Mr. Alexander Steele and his wife had also come into the room. Mrs. Steele offered to see to Miss Emily, and they left. I asked Mr. Alexander Steele to send for our physician, Mr. Carlstone. It was then that I asked Mrs. Watson to remove the broken crockery."

"And it was then you discovered the letter P?"

Miss Steele gave the magistrate a withering glance. "No, sir, it was not."

"Well, when was it then?"

"I retired to my room to quickly finish with my dressing, before Mr. Carlstone arrived. When I returned to my father's room, Mr. Carlstone was already there. It was he who pointed out the tile and asked that I send for the constable at once."

Mr. Alexander Steele was called next. He begged to be forgiven for his confusion, but hoped the magistrate would understand the reason. He had only arrived in Chester the day of his father's death, after a long and tiring journey from Italy. In addition to the fatigue there was also the emotion he had felt upon seeing his dear sisters for the first time in many years, as well as both the delight and shock he had felt upon casting his eyes upon his father — delight for he had long wished for the day when he would be reconciled with his dear parent, and shock to see his father in such an advanced state of ill health. He therefore only vaguely recalled the incident with the stable boy; of that dreadful moment when he realized his father was dead he recalled nothing at all.

"Very well, Mr. Steele, but should your memory improve, you are requested to come forward with your information. If there are no other witnesses ..."

A clerk pushed a note in the magistrate's direction.

"Samuel Pigeon? Who is that? What? Well, if you meant Sam the stable boy, why did you not say so, man?"

Before Sam was asked to come forward, another man appeared before the magistrate. This man and the magistrate remained huddled in discussion for several minutes. Constable Merriweather was summoned to join them, and the huddled conversation resumed. Then the magistrate called out, "Mr. George Hardwich, please come forward."

A sturdily built man with strong hands and sharp eyes pushed his way to the front of the room.

"Mr. Hardwich, you are the owner of the Black Lion public house, Northgate Row?"

"Yes, sir."

"And you have something to say concerning this matter?"

"Yes, sir, I do."

"Well, go ahead, man, say what you have to say, so we can all go to your establishment and have a glass of beer."

The assembly laughed at the jest, and the magistrate looked quite pleased.

"I was pouring out some beer a few days ago when some gentlemen entered the room. One of them in particular looked black as murder."

"Just tell us what you saw and heard, Mr. Hardwich. There is no need to embellish the facts with opinion."

"Very well, sir. So Mr. Halsey and his friends …"

"Are you referring to Mr. William Halsey or his older brother? Try to be precise, please."

"Mr. William Halsey, sir."

"Go on."

"So Mr. Halsey and his friends — and I can't say who the friends were, because they were strangers, sir, and they looker nearer to London gentlemen than from these parts."

"No one here expects you to say what you do not know. But get to the point, Mr. Hardwich. Tell us what you do know."

"So Mr. Halsey and his party sit down and while I'm giving them their beer I overhear parts of their conversation — not that I wish to listen to another man's conversation you understand, sir, but a man has ears."

"As do pitchers of ale, eh, Mr. Hardwich?" joked the magistrate a second time. He was a frequent visitor at the Black Lion. "But what does this have to do with the death of Mr. Steele?" he added, resuming his official demeanor. "Surely a man and friends are allowed to talk over their tankards of beer."

"Not that kind of talk, sir. The gentlemen were discussing the killing of The Miller of Dee, sir, and the talk was none too friendly."

"The Miller of Dee was Mr. Halsey's race horse?"

"Yes, sir. They were discussing who might have killed the horse, when I heard Mr. Halsey say, 'Who else could have done it? It must have been Thomas Steele.'"

William Halsey glanced over to where Emily Steele was seated. The young lady had turned very pale.

"Well, sir, a man is entitled to express an opinion," the magistrate continued. "I see no harm in that."

"But that is not all, sir. I then heard the young man say, and the hatred in his face nearly turned the blood in my veins to ice, 'He has stood in my way long enough. But he will not be able to do so for much longer!'"

There was a pause. Then the magistrate asked, "Did Mr. Halsey say anything else?"

"No, sir. He did not need to. His meaning was clear, to me and to the gentlemen who were with him."

"Perhaps that is true, Mr. Hardwich, but it is not yet clear to me. What exactly are you suggesting, sir?"

"Why, that Mr. Halsey intended to kill Mr. Steele."

The proceedings were interrupted by Miss Emily Steele, who collapsed onto the floor.

CHAPTER VI
THE PIGEON FLIES THE COOP

DURING THE HUBBUB THAT FOLLLOWED, Lord Lauferby found himself jostled not once but several times. But to do him credit, he ignored the insults to his coat and boots and forced his way through the crowd, to where his friend, Mr. Halsey, was standing, in a state of complete dismay.

"We must leave this place," said Lauferby, pulling at Halsey's sleeve.

"But Miss Steele—"

"She is being looked to. There is nothing for you to do."

Lord Lauferby was right on both accounts. The family physician, Mr. Carlstone, was administering hartshorn and the color was slowly returning to the young lady's cheeks. The lady's brother stood waiting to offer his arm, to escort her out of the room. Mr. Halsey therefore reluctantly followed Lord Lauferby through the crowd. But before they had gone far, they were stopped by Constable Merriweather.

"A word, Mr. Halsey."

"Yes, Constable?"

"I must ask you to return, sir. Believe me, Mr. Halsey, it will be much better if you come quietly, rather than make a scene before all these people."

William Halsey recognized the truth of those words. He said to his friend, "If you could send word to my parents, if I should be …"

"Do not be maudlin, Halsey. That publican's testimony was nothing more than gossip. No jury can be convinced by it. We shall dine together tonight."

The constable led Halsey back into the room. Lauferby was following behind them when he spotted Theo Bryght, who was standing at the far end of a corridor and inspecting the bottom part of a cupboard.

"What on earth are you doing, Bryght?" Lauferby called to him.

"I am looking for Sam," replied the Runner. He slammed the cupboard door shut and walked to where Lauferby was waiting. "He seems to have flown the coop."

"It is a pity Halsey did not fly with him."

"No, it is better to face the questions now — that is, of course, assuming Mr. Halsey is innocent."

If William Halsey found his situation to be distasteful, as he was led through the staring crowd, he was not alone. Constable Merriweather was perfectly in his element when it came to breaking up a brawl or scaring off young imps who were bothering a merchant's customers. But he was the old-fashioned sort, who believed there were different rules for members of the English gentry and the rest of the human race. Should a member of the titled class choose to do away with another person of rank, Constable Merriweather would rather look the other way and see the offending gentleman go free than see his own ideals go hang.

But when a member of the gentry harmed a member of Chester's merchant class, things became complicated. Chester was a mercantile town, and proud of it. Its merchants, who knew how to accurately assess the value of their goods, also knew how to accurately assess their own worth. One could not expect the town to stay quiet if there was a suspicion there had been foul play with one of their own. The constable therefore had a more pronounced frown upon his face than usual.

"It is all nonsense," the young man explained, after order had been restored and the inquest continued and he took the stand.

"You did not lose your temper, sir, when you discovered your horse was dead?" asked the magistrate.

"Of course, I did. That part is true. But who would not, I ask you?"

"I can think of very few men who would retain their composure," the magistrate agreed. Like the constable, he was unhappy with the way the inquest was going. Striking a balance between pursuing the truth and preserving the dignity of the gentry was a delicate task. "But is it true you said you thought Thomas Steele killed your horse?"

"It was all just talk. I was upset about the death of my horse and--"

"There was a rivalry between you and Mr. Steele, sir. The whole town knew about it."

"Naturally, we were rivals, since both of us intended to compete in the races this spring. But it was a rivalry that was confined to the stables, at least on my side. I have no idea why Mr. Hardwich thinks I intended to harm Mr. Steele."

"You did not threaten to remove Mr. Steele from your way?"

"I tell you, it was all just talk. Were you never young, sir? Did you never say more than you meant to do, when you were with friends?"

"Yes, sir, I was once young and about as foolish as they come. But my words were never followed by the death of my enemy. That needs some explaining. Who were those friends of yours?"

William Halsey looked down at his hands, hardly noticing they had clenched themselves into tight fists. "I should not like to drag them into this."

"Perhaps not, sir, but if they can assist you—"

"They cannot."

"I may be a better judge of that than you, sir."

"They cannot help me, I tell you."

The magistrate was no genius, but he was no fool either. A theory was beginning to form in his mind. It was not an original idea, but human behavior was seldom original either. He would be willing to bet a month's salary the "friends" were actually young Halsey's debtors, who had come to Chester to demand their money. The magistrate had not worked out his theory so far as to see what Halsey would accomplish by murdering Thomas Steele, but since he was not accustomed to being visited by brilliant flashes of insight he was not unduly bothered. If there was a trail that led between Mr. Halsey's debts and the murder of Thomas Steele, it would be found, eventually.

"Mr. Halsey, did you visit Mr. Steele on the day of his death?"

"No."

"Did you employ anyone to visit the deceased in your stead; Sam Pigeon perhaps?"

"No!"

"Were you anywhere near the vicinity of Number 10 Bridge Street Row on the day Mr. Steele died?"

Before Mr. Halsey could reply, a member of the jury — Mr. Martin Talbot, the owner of a dried goods store — stood up and said, "Take care, Mr. Halsey. I saw you talking with Sam in the alleyway behind Steele's home. You handed him something, a packet of some sort. I saw you do it."

"That is what I do not understand, Lauferby. If your friend wished to win the hand of the younger Miss Steele, why would he threaten to do away with the lady's father in a public place like the Black Lion?"

Theo Bryght and Lord Lauferby were walking along the Walls, which had the advantage of being deserted at that hour. The spirits of both of them were depressed, for the inquest had resulted in a verdict neither had anticipated — a verdict that William Halsey was guilty of poisoning Thomas Steele. Lord Lauferby could not believe his friend had poisoned Steele with his own hand; that a gentleman would employ an unsuspecting stable boy to do the deed for him was even more unthinkable.

"Come, Bryght, you were young once," he replied, pleading the cause of his friend. "Did you never let your tongue run loose when you should have kept it under lock and key?"

Theo Bryght accepted the reprimand. Lauferby knew the Runner's story and how his quarrel with his father had resulted in the loss of the income Bryght would have received as a younger son, not to mention his position in society as a clergyman. But that had been a quarrel over a matter of principle, a refusal to live a life of hypocrisy, for Bryght knew he was as suited to be a clergyman as to be a hairdresser. If a lady had been at stake, he liked to think that he would have played his hand more wisely.

Yet Lauferby had a point. It was the privilege of youth to make every mistake possible, and still hope and believe everything would work out right in the end.

"But if the thing Mr. Halsey handed to Sam was a letter for Miss Steele, as Mr. Halsey insisted at the inquest, we must hope your friend had the foresight to put a date on it and that Miss Steele kept it."

"I am certain she will do everything in her power to assist Halsey."

"In this instance, her ability to help may be limited. Love letters can be embarrassing."

Lord Lauferby kicked away some dead leaves that had fallen onto the path. "What shall I tell Halsey? Will you help him, Bryght?"

"If he wishes me to — and if Sir Richard wishes to retain my services for this new complication — yes, I will try to find out who murdered Thomas Steele."

"Will you come with me to the jail, to tell him?"

"You go," said Bryght. "I will meet you at the inn for supper."

Lord Lauferby trotted off. The Runner was glad to walk on alone. He wanted to think through the events of the morning, while the inquest was still fresh in his mind. There was something not right about this affair, but he could not put his finger on what was bothering him.

He could not say he was entirely surprised that William Halsey would be a suspect in the murder of Thomas Steele, at least in the beginning, when it was customary for the investigators to spread a wide net. But Bryght's instincts, upon meeting the young man, had told him that William Halsey was one of those pleasant, ineffectual younger sons of the gentry who were adequate in the drawing room and men's club, but lacked the ambition and conviction to make their mark on the wider spheres of life. In short, Bryght could see Halsey making a foolish threat when among his friends, but he could not believe Halsey had the gumption to do the actual deed. It was therefore unfortunate Halsey had chosen that particular day to send his young lady a missive, and even more unfortunate that someone had seen him hand the packet to Sam — if that was what had really happened.

What was more unfortunate was that Sam had disappeared; the boy could have verified Halsey's story. Even though a stable boy's testimony was not as valuable as that of a shopkeeper, it would perhaps have been enough to convince the jury that the so-called evidence offered by Mr. Hardwich and Mr. Talbot was slender and so there was still a reasonable doubt. The fact that the boy had bolted had been a factor in persuading the jury that Halsey was guilty.

The Runner, though, persisted in believing in the reasonable doubt that Halsey was innocent. It was possible Halsey had handed Sam not a love note but a packet containing poison, with instructions to deposit the contents in the pitcher in the sick room. That would certainly explain Sam's fright and subsequent flight. But Bryght did not think this scenario was true. He could see Sam delivering a love note, but he could not see the boy knowingly poison someone; he liked Sam and, again, he did not believe his instincts were wrong.

But why, then, had the jury been so willing to believe that both William Halsey and Sam had done the crime? Why could they not see that a stable boy would be terrified of any brush with the law and try to flee? There was obviously a piece to the Chester puzzle he was not yet familiar with, some grudge from a bygone day perhaps.

His steps had taken him to a section of the Wall called Morgan's Mount; here, his guidebook had told him, could sometimes be seen the ghosts of the Civil War's Cavaliers and their ladies, calmly promenading past the scene where fierce battles had been fought and lost. He did not see any ghosts, but the autumnal scene, with its abundant panoply of trees clothed in leafy robes of yellow and scarlet, put him in a melancholy frame of mind. Unlike the canal below, which had flowed beside the Walls for centuries before and would flow beside them for centuries to come, human life was fleeting. Someday there would be others, also with guidebooks in their hands, who would remark upon those gallant Cavaliers and their ladies, perhaps laughing at their elaborate costumes and manners, even while a new generation was waiting in the wings, ready to laugh at them and their own fashions.

And so he walked, until he came upon the next stop of a Chester visitor's tour, a place that had once been called Goblin Tower but was now more jestingly named Pemberton's Parlour, due to the semi-circular alcove that had been carved into the Tower's wall. He had not yet reached this alcove when he stopped, listened, and felt his heart skip a beat. A voice was emanating from inside the Tower, and if he had seen a ghost he could not have been more surprised.

"Really, Charlotte, I do think you might take more interest," the voice was saying. "The history of this place is most remarkable."

"I am sorry, Auntie. What were you saying?"

"I was telling you the story of Mr. Pemberton and his Parlour. But if the journey has tired you and you would prefer to return to our rooms …"

"Yes, I should like some tea. We can continue our circuit of the Walls tomorrow, if you like."

The Runner knew the two ladies would be leaving the recessed alcove at any moment. And for a moment he seriously considered leaping over the side of the Wall and taking cover in the grove below. Then he recalled the

Cavaliers who had stood on this spot before him. If they could stand up to the onslaught of the cannonballs of the Parliamentarians, he supposed he was cavalier enough to withstand this unexpected meeting with Lady Charlotte Ashe and her chaperon and aunt, Mrs. Seymour.

At first it seemed the two ladies might proceed in the direction of the Water Tower, and therefore not see the Runner. But then Mrs. Seymour said, "No, I think it is this way, Charlotte," and the two ladies turned.

Theo Bryght waited to be acknowledged, as was the rule when meeting an acquaintance of the female sex. For a few awkward moments it seemed Lady Ashe had decided not to renew their acquaintance, for they had not met under happy circumstances: Her husband, Lord Ashe, had been murdered, and much of her fortune had been squandered by her husband before he died. The Bow Street Runner had been called in to find the murderer; as for the fortune, the bulk of it had been irretrievably lost. No, he would not blame her if she should choose to forget those unhappy days, although he would be disappointed.

But then she smiled and nodded her head in his direction and said, "Mr. Bryght, how very nice to see you again. Auntie, you do remember Mr. Bryght from London, do you not?"

Mrs. Seymour gave the Runner a nod and a sour look. She had her own reasons for wanting to snub the Runner. In her opinion, it was his fault that her hopes of marrying off her widowed and orphaned niece to the very wealthy Lord March had not come to fruition. Although Charlotte had never said outright that this why she had refused Lord March's offer of marriage, Mrs. Seymour had muttered to herself more than once there was a reason why her niece had a perpetual fit of the mopes, and that reason could be found in the person of "that Runner from London."

"Have you come to Chester for business, Mr. Bryght, or to see the sights?" Lady Ashe continued.

"For business, my lady, though it would be my pleasure to be of service to you and Mrs. Seymour while you are here. Perhaps you would like to see the Cathedral. I hear it is very fine."

"Very kind of you, Mr. Bryght, I am sure," said Mrs. Seymour. "But we were just on our way back to our rooms. We have only arrived from Wales this morning, and we must not over-tire ourselves on our first day. Is that not what you were just now saying, Charlotte?"

"Yes, Auntie. But I was also saying I should like some tea. Would you care to join us, Mr. Bryght?"

Mr. Bryght would have liked very much to join Lady Ashe for tea, but a quick look at Mrs. Seymour told him that perhaps he should wait until the first storm had passed. He therefore declined, but he did accept an invitation to call on the two ladies after dinner, instead.

CHAPTER VII
WHISPERINGS ON BRIDGE STREET

WHEN THE STEELE FAMILY returned home after the inquest, Julia insisted on helping Emily to her bed.

"I am fine now. Truly, I am," Emily protested.

"Yes, and you shall feel even better after you have had a rest," Julia insisted.

When the door was closed behind them, Julia revealed the reason for her insistence, in a whisper. "Emily — may I still call you Emily?"

"Of course, Julia."

"And may I still hope you wish to be my friend?"

"Yes, but why are you whispering?"

"Did you not hear? Did you not see what happened at the inquest?"

"Mr. Halsey was accused of poisoning my father."

"He was not the only one. What did your sister mean, Emily, when she said someone could have put poison in the glass when Alexander was in the room?"

"Oh, Julia, you must not think anyone in this house suspects Alexander!"

"Not you, my dear. You are too sweet and good."

"Not Mary, either! It was the magistrate who inferred this evil from her words."

"She did not protest."

"No, she did not."

Emily sank down upon a chair, suddenly exhausted. It was true. Mary had not protested. She had been puzzled by this at the time. But the events that had followed had driven the incident out of her mind.

"You see, you are tired, my dear," said Julia. "Let me help you take off your hat."

"Perhaps I do need to rest."

"Yes, this inquest has been a great shock to us all. But, Emily, may I ask of you a favor?"

"Of course."

"Alexander and I are strangers here. Not just to Chester, we are strangers to England, as well. We have no family and no friends, other than you and Miss Steele. Perhaps I misunderstood Miss Steele's actions this morning. It is so easy to misunderstand when you are a stranger. But, Emily, you I do not misunderstand. Alexander and I can trust you, is this not so?"

"Julia, how can you ask such a thing? Alexander is my brother."

"Yes, you feel the connection. You two are very alike — warm, generous."

"Please do not be too severe in your opinion of Mary. She is also capable of deep feelings, powerful feelings, although she does not often express them openly."

"That is why I fear her. It is the ones who are deep, yet closed, who can bring so much sorrow into the world."

"Do not think that, Julia. It just takes Mary time to become accustomed to new people. And it has been such a shock, first Father's death and then this inquest."

"Even before, on that very first day, I could see it in her eyes. She does not like me, or Alexander. I know it. You know it, as well, which is why you are now silent. Is that not so, my sweet child?"

Emily did not reply. She did not have the strength to defend her sister. For how could she say Julia was wrong when she too had felt from a young age that Mary had tolerated her but never really liked her? She too had felt the coldness, the always critical eye. Yet she had never seen Mary ever intentionally harm anyone. And even though she was a strict mistress, she was a fair one and so the servants generally stayed on. Emily tried to explain all this to Julia; that this house had never been a warm home, a loving home, but it had never been a cruel home, either. Therefore, there was no reason to be alarmed.

"My poor angel," said Julia, "do you really not see?"

"See what?"

"We have every reason to be alarmed. All of us. Except for one."

"Whatever do you mean?"

"Someone murdered your father. If it was not your Mr. Halsey, then the person must be someone in this house."

While Julia was speaking with Emily, Mary Steele sat at her housekeeping table and counted out Mrs. Watson's wages. After Mrs. Watson had expressed her thanks, and secured the coins in her handkerchief, she remained standing before the mistress of the house.

"Well?"

"I was wondering, Miss Steele, about my box of alphabet tiles."

"What about them?"

"I would like to have them back, seeing how they belonged to my mother."

"You must speak to the constable. I believe the box is still in his care."

"Yes, Miss, I shall do that. But if you could also put in a word, Miss Steele, I am sure it would help to move matters along."

"I will see what I can do."

When Mrs. Watson still did not leave the room, Mary asked a second time, "Well?"

"It was not Mister Alexander who put the poison in the glass, Miss, or Sam. I thought you would like to know."

"How can you know that, Mrs. Watson?"

"I gave Mr. Steele a drink from that glass after Mister Alexander left the room, when I brought up the hot water bottle."

"Perhaps the poison was already in the glass."

"If it was, it wasn't there when Mr. Steele took his drink. I rinsed the glass and wiped it clean before I poured out the ale. I always did this after that stable boy paid your father a visit. Sam's a nice boy, but he's not particular about where he spits."

"Yes, you were a great one for cleanliness, Mrs. Watson. It was one of the things I appreciated about you. But the poison could have been in the pitcher. Have you thought of that?"

"I had no need to, Miss Steele. You see I also took a glass of ale, to keep Mr. Steele company. And here I am — the picture of health."

While spreading her hands to call attention to the robust picture of health that was Mrs. Watson, one of those hands turned into a gesture of an outreached hand and an upturned palm. Mary Steele snapped shut the strongbox where the money was kept for the household expenses and locked it with her key. "Yes, Mrs. Watson, you are the picture of health, and may that good health continue. Who is there?"

The two women turned as one toward the door, which they both now saw had not been completely closed.

"Begging your pardon, Miss Steele," said a man, bowing his way into the room, "but Mr. Carlstone had to attend to a patient and so he asked me to deliver this powder. It is a mild sedative, should Miss Emily need it."

"Thank you, Mr. Willows," said Mary, refusing to take the packet, "but I have already given Miss Emily one of my father's powders. We have plenty on hand."

Mr. Willows, the apothecary who had a shop further down the Row, bowed again and followed Mrs. Watson, who was already making a hasty retreat out the door.

"Well?" asked Alexander, when Julia returned to their room.

"Emily suspects nothing. If that woman and her tiles had not—"

"Hush. There is no use crying over that."

"The whole thing is absurd. Whoever heard of a man in the throes of death grabbing a child's alphabet tiles and spelling out the cause of his death?"

"Yes, it is absurd. It is like the child who tries to be too clever. But we are also clever, Julia."

"I hope so, Alexander. I hope so very much."

CHAPTER VIII
A VOTE FOR CHESTER

BEFORE THEO BRYGHT RETURNED to his rooms at the Bear and Billet to dress for dinner, he decided to pay a visit to the Roodee. He did not require an introduction from the Halsey family to make plausible his presence. A visit to Chester without a visit to the racecourse, which claimed to be the oldest one in England, dating its first horse race to the days of King Henry VIII, could be viewed, in some quarters, as similar to neglecting to see the Pyramids while touring Egypt.

Of course, his interest in the track was both a professional and a sporting one, and so before climbing down from the Walls he took a few moments to survey the scene.

The course lay at the western-most end of Chester — in Roman times it had been the town's harbor — and beyond it was an open vista that provided a clear view into Wales. At the northern end of the course were a few buildings, presumably the stables and lodgings for visiting jockeys and stablemen, who would descend upon Chester in the spring, during the racing season. As for the racecourse itself, besides one small clump of trees sprouting up in the middle of the sea of green grass, the track was level and unobstructed.

This suggested two things. Either the killer of The Miller of Dee was a reckless man who did not care if he was seen sprinting across the open course before reaching safety, since he could have been observed by anyone who happened to be standing on this section of the Walls, or the killer was someone who was well known at the course, and therefore to see him ambling on the grass would not arouse suspicion.

Having satisfied himself that he had seen all there was to be observed from this vantage point, the Runner proceeded to the stables. The majority of the stalls were empty, but one held a magnificent specimen. Pitch black in color, haughty in demeanor, the horse must be Cavalier, he decided, the now orphaned horse of Thomas Steele.

"Aye, that's Cavalier," said a gravelly voice.

Theo Bryght turned. An elderly but spry-looking man had soundlessly sidled up beside him.

"And you must be Old Peter."

"Aye, that I am."

"Your pipe is cold, sir. May I offer you some of my tobacco?"

Although Theo Bryght did not usually smoke, he found it useful to carry with him a pouch of good quality tobacco. The business of filling and lighting a pipe took time, which gave him an excuse for engaging in conversation. Old Peter took the tobacco, but he was not the typical garrulous old man Bryght had hoped to find.

"It is a fine horse," said the Runner. "What will happen to Cavalier now?"

"Aye, that's a fine question."

"Anyone come to inquire about buying it?"

"Other than you, sir?" the old stable hand asked with a sly smile.

"What makes you think I wish to buy the horse?"

"Maybe the way you haven't any other reason to be nosing around where you have no business to be, sir."

"I see there is no pulling the wool over your eyes," said the Runner, laughing. "What can you tell me? Does the family plan to keep the horse, or sell it?"

"I don't know, sir, on account of the fact that the will hasn't been read yet. Maybe Mr. Steele didn't leave the horse to his family. Maybe he left Cavalier to young Sam, or maybe he left Cavalier to Mr. William Halsey!" Old Peter laughed heartily but kept one eye screwed on his visitor.

Was this a hint Old Peter wished to talk about The Miller of Dee, the Runner wondered, or was the elderly man still eying him with suspicion, not entirely believing that he wished to purchase Mr. Steele's horse? It was impossible to know; he therefore responded with a feint.

"Ah yes, the will. I hear Mr. Steele left behind two unmarried daughters. Surely they do not interest themselves in horse racing."

"You are forgetting, sir, about the young Mr. Steele."

"I have not heard about a young Mr. Steele."

"Nor have most people. He was away in Eetalee for twenty and more years, so people say. But he came back to Chester the day old Mr. Steele died."

"That was very convenient for him, coming into his inheritance so soon after his arrival home."

"So some people say." Old Peter took a long pull on his pipe. "Your tobacco is very fine, sir, but my throat is dry. Tis a pity I have nothing to wet it with."

Theo Bryght removed a flask from his coat pocket and poured out a capful of the brandy. "To your health," he said, raising the capful to his own lips, while handing the flask to the old man.

"And to yours, sir." Old Peter took a generous drink. "If the family should ask, should I say you're interested in Cavalier, sir?"

"Not yet. I have heard this stable is an unlucky one."

"How so, sir?"

"You should know better than me. First The Miller of Dee was killed. By the way, how was The Miller killed?"

"Poisoned, sir. Hemlock, they said it was, mixed in with the poor horse's hay. Very sad it was, too. The Miller was a devil of a horse."

"And then Mr. Steele was poisoned."

"Aye, very sad," Old Peter agreed, but with less feeling than he had expressed for the dead horse.

"And now there is Sam."

"Sam, sir?"

"The boy has gone missing, has he not? Or are you hiding him here?"

"I've not seen him since this morning, when he set off for the inquest, with Mr. Halsey."

"There you are then. If he is not here and he is not with Mr. Halsey, where is he? If this were a horse race, I would place my money on a horse named Poison."

The flask fell out of the old man's hands. Fortunately, by this time the flask was almost empty and so not too much brandy was wasted.

"Not Sam. Who would want to poison young Sam?" the elderly man fairly pleaded.

Two men were already seated in the Bear and Billet's private sitting room when Theo Bryght entered. One was Lord Lauferby. The other man he knew only by reputation, as who did not? Even in an age filled to the brim with eccentricity and excess, "Mad Jack" Mytton stood out. It was said he was so fond of hunting that he would set out in the dead of night, in the dead of winter, to catch his prey — wearing nothing other than his gun. It was said he allowed his favorite horse to wander freely about his manor house — and make its bed in the best place in the entire estate, in front of the drawing room fire. It was said he would accept any bet — he once tried to see if a horse pulling a carriage could jump over a tollgate; it could not — and brush off the loss, which often included a few broken ribs in addition to vast sums of money, like ordinary men brushed off a piece of lint from their coat's sleeve. It was said ... But there sat the man, larger than life and more than able to speak for himself.

The introductions were made and Theo Bryght took a seat at the table. If the number of empty bottles on that table was an indication, Mad Jack had not been idle while waiting for him to arrive.

"Mr. Bryght, I am not overly fond of the law," Mad Jack drawled, waving his glass in the direction of the Runner's face. "But if you can find The Miller's killer, like you found the carriage carrying Miss Stopfield and that dragoon of hers to the Scottish border, I shall be honored to count you among my friends."

"I thank you, sir, but you are under a misapprehension. I have never had the pleasure of meeting any lady by the name of Miss Stopfield."

Mad Jack gave the Runner a broad wink. "I like a man who can hold his tongue. But Miss Stopfield is my cousin, sir. I have heard the story of her thwarted elopement — and your part in the story — more times than I care to tell you." Mytton then turned to Lord Lauferby and said, "Miss Stopfield was quite taken with her rescuer. It is the opinion of many she would not have minded galloping on to Scotland with this Runner!"

While the young lord politely laughed, Theo Bryght inwardly groaned. The memory of Miss Stopfield — a young lady who was all giggles and ribbons and curls — was not a particularly pleasant one. The hours he had spent in her company, while escorting her back to her father's home in London, had been some of the most excruciating hours of his life.

Fortunately, some shouts from the public room recalled Mad Jack to the second reason why he was in Chester, which was to help influence the local elections. Removing some coins from his money pouch, he said, with a wink, "One drink, one vote — that is the way to win an election. There's no need for all this speechifying and promising the lower classes this and that."

"And after the election?" asked Bryght.

"After the election? They can buy their own drinks, after that!"

While Mad Jack was in the other room, standing drinks for the entire crowd, Theo Bryght mentioned to Lauferby that he had paid a visit to the stables at the Roodee. In answer to Lauferby's raised eyebrow, he explained, "I learned nothing about The Miller's death, but I do know Sam is not hiding there. I think we can believe Old Peter about that. Sam has not turned up here, has he?"

"No," replied Lord Lauferby. "Have you an idea where the boy could be?"

"I suppose he could easily find a hiding place underneath the Rows. I have found out some of the shop owners still use the underground vaults to store their merchandise. But if that is where he is hiding, it will be difficult to find him. He would see and hear us long before we would see him."

Their conversation was interrupted by a shout from the other room. Theo Bryght went to the door of their private sitting room and opened it. In the crowded public room, a new round of drinks was being poured, amid much laughter.

"And who will you vote for in the election?" Mad Jack was roaring from his perch on top of a table.

"Lord Grosvenor!" the men yelled as one.

"I cannot hear you! I must be deaf in one ear!"

"Lord Grosvenor!" they yelled again.

"Perkins, give these men another drink," called out Mad Jack. "If that is as loud as they can crow, these roosters must have a hole in their gullets."

Although this was not the Runner's idea of the proper way to campaign for an election, he knew he could not censure Mad Jack for either the man's cynicism or his tactics for winning votes. A similar scene, this one for the opposing candidate, was most likely taking place at another one of the town's other public houses at this very moment.

The Runner was about to re-close the door when he saw someone beckon to Mad Jack, who jumped down from the table with an exuberant leap. He watched, fascinated, while the campaigner's exultant grin turned into a look of bemused surprise, which was quickly followed by one of extreme shock. This, in turn, was replaced by a scowl so fierce the man who had been whispering in Mad Jack's ear backed away several paces, apparently afraid himself at the powerful effect of his words.

When Mad Jack saw the Runner standing in the doorway, he rushed to him and pushed Bryght back into the sitting room, slamming the door behind them.

"I'll kill him!" yelled Mad Jack. "And if you try to stop me, I'll kill you too!"

Theo Bryght calmly poured out a fresh drink and handed it to Mytton. "I am a Bow Street Runner. Therefore, I will try to stop you, as I would try to stop any murderer, I promise you that. But to make this a more sporting contest, perhaps you would like to tell me who you intend to kill, besides me."

"That Halsey scoundrel has made a fool of both of us." Mad Jack glanced over at where Lord Lauferby was sitting, considering for a moment as to whether or not he should amend his statement to also include the young man. But a look at Lauferby's mauve and canary-yellow striped waistcoat made him decide there was no need; the young lord, in his opinion, was already a fool — a foolish young tulip from London.

Lord Lauferby, who could return a haughty stare as well as anyone, put his quizzing glass to his eye and said, "That is a harsh thing to say about a man, sir — especially a man who is in jail and therefore cannot demand satisfaction."

"Are you implying I am a coward?"

Before more heated words could be exchanged, Bryght stood between the two men and said, "No one is accusing you of anything, Mytton, except that you are too slow in telling your tale. Why do you wish to kill William Halsey?"

"He murdered my horse. He killed The Miller of Dee."

For a moment, all the Runner could do was stare. Then he said, "Why on earth would he do that?"

"To prevent his creditors from seizing the horse — the men who helped him buy The Miller, in the first place."

"That makes no sense. If his creditors were willing to take the horse instead of cash, why not give the horse to them?"

"Because it would become known in town," replied Mad Jack. "Apparently the scoundrel decided to sacrifice the horse to save his reputation, so he could marry that silk mercer's daughter. I'll kill him!"

Since Mad Jack had sunk into a seat by the table and begun to pour himself another drink, the Runner surmised it was safe to leave the man with Lord Lauferby while he sought out the person who had divulged this new piece of information. The public room was still crowded and, if anything, the clouds of smoke had grown even denser. But the man Bryght was looking for was still in the room, and he did not object when the Runner asked him to step outside.

The difference between the crowded room and the empty Row was great. Whereas one was hot and noisy, the other was cool and silent. The Row was also dark, very dark, and not for the first time did the Runner consider that a Chester Row was as good a place for a murder as any dark alleyway in London. But his companion, who appeared to be a respectable middle-aged citizen of the town, did not seem to be looking for a fight, at least not at the moment.

"I am a Bow Street Runner from London. I have been summoned to Chester to investigate the murder of The Miller of Dee. I hear you know something about it."

"I told the other gentleman all I know, sir," said the man.

"Perhaps you would like to tell me your name and how you came to know your information."

"My name is no secret in this town. I have a shop on Bridge Street Row. You will see my name on the sign. Thaddeus Jones."

"And what makes you think, Mr. Jones, The Miller of Dee was killed by its owner?"

"I saw Mr. Halsey at the racecourse."

"You were at the stable?"

"No, sir. I am interested in the stars. I often take my telescope to the Roodee on a clear night and gaze up at the heavens and chart the course of the stars and planets. The racecourse is a dark and open space that suits my purpose admirably."

"What happened on the night The Miller was killed?"

"I arrived not long after midnight. I set up my telescope and charting papers and proceeded with my observations. It was about an hour later, I would say, that I heard footsteps approaching."

"Could you see the person's face?"

"No, but I recognized the coat. I am a tailor and haberdasher by profession, sir, and it was I who made the coat for Mr. Halsey. We had a disagreement about the number of capes. I cannot see the back of that coat without feeling I was right. But of course I could not insist that Mr. Halsey accept my opinion."

"And so you saw Mr. Halsey's coat walk across the racecourse?"

"Yes, and then he entered the stable."

"He did not see you?"

"No. It was a dark night — there was no moon — and I was sitting on the ground."

"The metal of your telescope might have caught a glint from Mr. Halsey's lantern."

"He was not carrying a lantern. Or if he was, it was not lit."

"How long was Mr. Halsey inside the stable?"

"I cannot say exactly. I returned my attention to my telescope and my charts."

"You did not think it odd that Mr. Halsey was visiting the stable at such a late hour?"

"I think many things in this world are odd, but it is not my place to question the actions of the gentry."

"Did you see Mr. Halsey leave the stable?"

"No. But there is more than one door. He may have left by a door in the back."

"Were you still at the Roodee when the horse became ill?"

"No, I can only make my observations for an hour or two, since I must be up early in the morning to open my shop."

"Mr. Jones, why have you waited until this evening to divulge what you saw?"

"Well, sir, it seems to me this Mad Jack Mytton is a noisy fellow who may not mean any harm, but who could cause trouble for the Halsey family without his intending to. Sending for you, for example — what good will it do anyone if you were to discover it was William Halsey who murdered the horse? He may have been a fool to do so, but it was his property. He did not harm anyone. And he is in enough trouble now that he has been accused of murdering Thomas Steele. That is why I suggested to Mr. Mytton it would be best to halt the investigation concerning The Miller. I do not know if he will accept my suggestion — I seem to lack the gift of oratory persuasion — and so I present it to you, sir, as well. Go back to London. Let what is dead and gone remain buried."

CHAPTER IX
AN IMPOSSIBLE SITUATION

WHEN THEO BRYGHT ARRIVED at the inn where Lady Ashe and Mrs. Seymour were staying, the two ladies had finished their dinner and were drinking coffee with their two dinner companions, a baronet and his wife, who were also staying at the inn. The Runner's appearance, which was greeted with frosty condescension by all except Lady Ashe, gave the baronet and his wife an opportunity to say their goodnights, since they had to make an early start in the morning.

When Charlotte excused herself for a few moments, and Theo Bryght found himself sitting alone with Mrs. Seymour, he wondered if this was how the early Christians felt, while sitting with the lions in their dens.

"I will not be silent," Mrs. Seymour fumed with decision, as though such a possibility was ever really a question. "I do not approve of your visiting my niece, and I do not know what people will say when they discover you are here. If you were a gentleman, in manners if not in actual fact, you would make your excuses when Lady Ashe returns and leave Chester at once."

"I thank you for your frank advice, Mrs. Seymour. But perhaps we should let Lady Ashe be the judge, especially since I am in Chester to help a young gentleman who has been accused of murder."

"Murder?"

"Who has been accused of murder?" asked Charlotte, who had returned to the room.

"I would willingly tell you the entire story, Lady Ashe, but I believe Mrs. Seymour is tired and prefers that I take my leave."

The Runner waited for his words to do their work. He knew from prior experience that Mrs. Seymour, although a most admirable woman in other areas, had one prominent failing: an incurable appetite for gossip. Although she had not been at all pleased when murder — and its companion, scandal — had arrived at her niece's door, in the form of the murder of Viscount Ashe, the Runner correctly assumed that someone else's murder would hold no such negative connotations.

And so the good woman sat, with two terrible forces struggling within her: a noble desire to show the Runner immediately to the door, before he could make further inroads into her niece's all too vulnerable heart, versus a consuming need to keep the Runner in his chair until every last thrilling detail had been devoured.

At last the battle was decided.

"Charlotte, Mr. Bryght has no coffee. Where are your manners, my dear? And you must try some of this delicious cake, Mr. Bryght. Or perhaps you would prefer a glass of port while you tell us all about this horrid thing that has happened."

"I congratulate you, sir," Lady Ashe said under her breath, as she handed Theo Bryght his coffee. "You have made a conquest."

"Only one?"

"We shall see."

And so the Runner told the two ladies almost all he knew. When he mentioned the name of the young man, Charlotte said with surprise, "Not the Halsey family that lives at Stanley Hall?"

"Yes, William Halsey is the younger son. Do you know them?"

"Lady Halsey was a childhood friend of my mother. They went to the same school. She and Sir Richard visited us at Hopewell, after my grandfather died. Do you not remember, Auntie? Lady Halsey brought some letters that had been written by my mother, which she had kept."

"We should have called upon them, Charlotte. I hope they will not hear we have been in Chester."

"Perhaps we should extend our stay, Auntie."

Mrs. Seymour gave the Runner another scowl, angry that she had allowed herself to fall into this new trap. The last thing she wanted was for Charlotte to remain in the same town as the Runner, even if it meant offending the Halseys.

Meanwhile, Theo Bryght was continuing with his tale, trying to maintain a professional mien when the truth was that he would have been content to sip his coffee in silence and merely gaze in adoration at the woman sitting beside him.

"Do you believe the two incidents are linked, Mr. Bryght?" Charlotte asked, after the Runner had finished recounting the facts of the case.

"What is your opinion, Lady Ashe?"

"It is interesting that the cause of both murders was poison."

"Yes, although the fact that it was poison both times is perhaps too obvious, as if the murderer of Mr. Steele wished to establish a link that is not truly there."

"Then you do not believe Mr. Halsey committed both crimes?"

"I am not yet convinced he committed even one."

"You believe then that Mr. Steele was murdered by his son, Mr. Alexander Steele?"

"I do not yet have an opinion. But I do know Alexander Steel could not have killed The Miller of Dee, since he was not in England at the time. It is also doubtful he would have heard the horse was poisoned and that Miss Emily Steele wished to marry William Halsey, against her father's wishes, and planned his own crime accordingly. There would not have been time."

"I agree with Mr. Bryght," Mrs. Seymour purred. "I do not think the two incidents are linked. I also do not believe Mr. Steele spelled out the word 'poison' before his death."

"Your reason, ma'am?"

"Well, think of it," said Mrs. Seymour, supremely flattered by the Bow Street Runner's interest in her opinion. "There is Mr. Steele, already a half-paralyzed man, in the agonized throes of death, and what does he do? He calmly picks out alphabet tiles from the jumble and arranges them nicely on his bedside table. It would be as if I or Charlotte were to calmly stitch the letters on our needlepoint canvases. I do not refer to the length of time, mind you, but the mental processes. Who could think of spelling at such a time?"

"Then how did the tile get in his hand?"

"Someone put it there!"

"Who?"

The ladies were silent.

"It could not have been Mr. Halsey," said Charlotte. "No one has said they saw him inside the house."

"True," said the Runner. "But Mr. Halsey might have employed a proxy."

"You mean the boy, Sam?" A look of worry clouded Charlotte's brow. "Mr. Bryght, do you think the boy is involved in this crime, somehow? Is he in danger?"

"He is involved, whether he knowingly allowed himself to be involved or not, and whether he truly knows something or not. Therefore, I think he is in great danger. The question is, has he found himself a safe hiding place, until the danger has passed?"

"I cannot believe Mr. Halsey is involved with either incident," said Charlotte.

"Because your mother and his mother were friends?"

Charlotte blushed at the rebuke. Before she could say anything, though, the Runner continued, "But I agree with you, Lady Ashe. Poison is usually not a gentleman's crime. It is more often done by the ladies. Let us therefore put aside Mr. Halsey for the time being. Who does that leave for a killer of Mr. Steele?"

"His family," Charlotte said, "although that seems too horrible to believe."

"Let us list them: Mr. Alexander Steele, Miss Mary Steele, and Miss Emily Steele. There is also the wife of Mr. Steele, whose given name, I believe, is Julia."

"Do not forget the nurse, Mr. Bryght," Mrs. Seymour chimed in. "It was poisoning, do not forget, and who better to administer the dose than a nurse?"

"I am in your debt, Mrs. Seymour," he said, hoping he was not doing it too brown. "I had not thought of that aspect of the case. We most certainly will add Mrs. Watson to the list."

"I do not suppose we should suspect the servants," said Charlotte.

"On the contrary, my lady, I find it beneficial to list anyone who could have performed the deed. I am hampered only by my lack of familiarity with the Steele household. It is a pity I know no one in Chester who has a servant like your maid Ella. I am sure Ella could find out everything we should wish to know."

"I hope you do not mean you wish to employ Ella as your assistant, Mr. Bryght." A warning signal had sounded in Mrs. Seymour's head. It was one thing to talk over a murder in the sitting room, and quite another to become actually involved in the work.

"Why not, Auntie, if it will help to clear Mr. Halsey's name? And think of that poor boy, who is very likely shivering in some dark cellar at this very moment. I hope he at least found some food for his supper."

"Ella comes from a respectable farming family, and we are responsible for her," replied Mrs. Seymour. "I do not mean to cast aspersion on your own family, Mr. Bryght; I am sure your mother was a fine woman. But Ella shall not do the work of a Bow Street Runner — spying through keyholes and playing the role of the saucy maid to pry out information from the valet and the grocer's boy and who knows who else. And that is my final word."

The Runner tried not to smile. Mrs. Seymour could not know his mother had been the daughter of a duke and the wife of an earl, and therefore it would have been exceedingly difficult to lower her standing in the eyes of the world. But that was the point, and he had to concede that Mrs. Seymour's view was the one that was correct. A Lady who did something disgraceful was still a Lady, while a compromised farmer's daughter would not be allowed to retain even that humble status.

"I apologize for having mentioned it, ma'am," he therefore said. "I shall have to find another way to become acquainted with the household."

"Yes, you shall," said Charlotte, whose mood had suddenly changed, and not for the better. "I was not thinking before. We cannot allow Ella to become involved in this ... business."

Mrs. Seymour was appeased, although she was the only one in the room who appeared to be happy. The Runner, whose profession had trained him to be sensitive to the depths of meaning that could be hidden within even a single word, had noticed the sudden chill that hung in the air.

"May I offer you more coffee, Mr. Bryght?" Mrs. Seymour asked.

"No, thank you. I must be going. May I write to you, Lady Ashe, to tell you how this incident has been resolved?"

"I should be very grateful if you would, Mr. Bryght."

After the Runner left, Charlotte retired to her room. But she did not go to bed. Instead, she sat at the dressing table, brushing her hair in a desultory manner. If only it were as easy to remove the tangled thoughts from her mind. The evening had not gone as she had hoped. But how could it have been otherwise? She now saw that a life *with* the Bow Street Runner was impossible, because the life *of* a Bow Street Runner was impossible. How could she have thought she would be happy spending her days running after murderers, worming her way into other people's homes and lives, trying to ferret out their secrets? It was no better than being a spy, which was something very low, indeed.

She gave her hair another vigorous pull with the brush. If only she could say to the man, "Here is my money and my estate, it is yours if you will leave London and give up your profession and come to live with me in Yorkshire. We can be happy." But that was the problem; she knew that a man like Theo Bryght would not be happy with such an arrangement, living off the wealth of a woman, even if that woman was his wife.

Neither would she. She had too much of her grandfather's blood pulsing through her veins. Although the age admired the man of leisure, the man who devoted his time and his intelligence to trivial matters such as the cut of his coat or the cut of a joint of beef, her admiration was for people like her grandfather, people who had started from humble beginnings and created something productive and profitable with their own hands. Her grandfather had gone to Jamaica as a young man, he had worked and struggled. Then his efforts were rewarded. His sugar plantation became successful and he became a wealthy man. In his later years, after he returned to England, he had been accepted into the drawing rooms of the county's established families. He had raised himself up, both financially and socially. And at the end of his life he had looked back with satisfaction at all he had accomplished.

A Bow Street Runner could not do the same. He would never be accepted socially. She would not care, perhaps. But could she disappoint her grandfather again? Although he had been dead for several years, his memory still occupied a precious place in her heart and mind. He was the only parent she had ever really known, since both her parents had died of the fever in Jamaica when she was young. How many times had he told her, "This is all for you, Charlotte. And you shall raise our family even higher." What would he say if he knew his only grandchild was in love with someone who earned his living by looking through keyholes?

She took out her anger and disappointment on her hair, once again brushing it with all her might. Then the clock chimed the half hour, reminding her she had something else to worry her. Her maid Ella, usually so reliable, had disappeared after dinner. It was utterly unlike the girl, but there it was. Ella was nowhere to be found.

Charlotte went over to the window, which faced onto the street, to see if anyone was about. A cloaked figure was hurrying in the direction of the inn. Yes, it was Ella.

A few minutes later there was the sound of footsteps running up the stairs. Then the door opened and Ella entered the room.

"Begging your pardon, my lady," Ella said, hurriedly removing her cloak and bonnet. "Shall I bring up the hot water?"

"Where have you been, Ella?"

"I had rather not say, my lady."

"I am sure you had rather not, but you will tell me, all the same."

"I was having tea, my lady, with an acquaintance, and we forgot the time."

"I was not aware you knew anyone in Chester."

"I did not, my lady, not before today. But while you and Mrs. Seymour were taking a walk around the Walls, I went to the inquest for the gentleman that was murdered."

"Mr. Steele?"

"Yes, my lady. That was where I met Margaret, my lady. Margaret is a parlor maid in the house."

"You have been drinking tea in the Steele house, with the servants?"

"Yes, my lady. It is a most respectable house, my lady, even though there has been a murder in it. And the servants are so low and upset, especially Margaret, who is a Yorkshire girl, my lady, and does not have another soul from home to talk to in this town. So I let her talk to me, seeing how I am a Yorkshire girl, too, and oh, my lady, she is so afraid the murderer is still in the house — despite the fact they have put a young gentleman in jail. I was almost scared out of my wits, myself, from the way she and the other servants were carrying on. I think it is the shock, my lady, and I told the cook to let Margaret and the others have some nice warm milk before they go to sleep. But can you believe it, they are all afraid to taste a thing, for fear there is poison in it!"

"That was a very sensible suggestion, on your part. But you know better than anyone, Ella, one cannot believe everything one hears in the servants' quarters. Please do not repeat anything you have seen or heard to anyone else."

"Yes, my lady, but …"

Ella, though always respectful, was usually not at a loss for words. Charlotte was therefore surprised by this unexpected silence. "If something is truly bothering you, please tell me what it is."

"Thank you, my lady. I only thought Mr. Bryght ought to know. I saw him at the inquest, my lady, and so I thought he must be in Chester investigating the murder."

"What should Mr. Bryght know?"

"Mr. Steele may be in danger."

"Mr. Steele? The son who has just returned from Italy?"

"Yes, my lady. And his wife, Mrs. Steele. Margaret says Mrs. Steele sits at the table, white as a ghost, and puts only the smallest morsel of food in her mouth. That is how frightened she is."

Charlotte studied the girl. Ella had been her personal maid for several years. She knew there was not much in this world that could frighten Ella, who was made from sturdy, down-to-earth Yorkshire stock. Yet there was still a trace of fear in the girl's eyes now.

It was said that sometimes evil, when lodged in a certain place, could be felt, as a tangible presence, like a coming storm could be felt before it broke. Was that what Ella had felt, what the others were feeling? Charlotte thought of Mrs. Steele, newly arrived in a foreign country, having to confront first the death of her husband's father and now this fear that a poisoner still lurked in their midst. Perhaps it was nonsense, but what if it were true? Theo Bryght had said the stable boy had already disappeared, most likely because he knew something he would have been better off not knowing. Had Mrs. Steele or Mr. Steele seen or heard something, which now placed their lives in danger?

Charlotte shuddered. She knew from her own sad past what it was like to come face to face with a killer. It was only because someone — Theo Bryght — had bothered to "worm" his way into her life and the lives of her late husband's acquaintances and ferret out their secrets that she was still alive today.

"Ella, would you go back to that house? Do you think you could return to the Steele house and offer to help out there for a few days?"

"I think they would not mind the extra help, seeing how everyone is so out of sorts. But why do you wish me to go there, my lady?"

"Mr. Bryght, the Bow Street Runner, will be able to tell you what to do, better than I can."

"Shall I be staying on alone, my lady, or will you and Mrs. Seymour be staying longer in Chester, too?"

"We shall stay in Chester as long as Mr. Bryght needs you to stay."

Charlotte continued to brush out her hair, while Ella laid out her lady's bedclothes. Every once in a while the maid glanced over at the mirror. Nothing about her mistress had changed, externally. But something told her the gloom that had hung over her mistress's life for the past several months was about to lift.

CHAPTER X
WHERE THERE IS A WILL

WITH ELLA ENSCONCED IN the Steele home as an additional parlor maid, Theo Bryght felt free to spend the next day pursuing his inquiries at the Roodee. When he arrived at the racecourse, the first thing he saw was Cavalier. To his surprise, he saw that Mad Jack Mytton was guiding the horse around the track, expertly handling the animal.

The trainer and jockey, who were watching the progress of the horse from the side of the track, both turned when the Runner climbed down to the turf. But a nod from Old Peter was enough to admit Bryght into this exclusive club.

"You have competition, sir," said Old Peter, nodding in the direction of Mad Jack. "That one knows the racing business."

They continued to watch as Mad Jack coaxed the horse around the final curve.

"Sam is not here?" Bryght whispered.

Old Peter shook his head.

After Mad Jack dismounted, he returned Cavalier to its trainer, Young Peter, saying, "You have done your job well, sir."

Young Peter's face fairly glowed as he led the horse back to the stable, with the jockey walking beside him.

"Cavalier has fire in his belly," Mad Jack said to Old Peter, "but he is not The Miller of Dee. What happened to my horse, old man? I want the truth. You can talk freely before this person."

"Aye, we are acquainted," replied Old Peter, nodding in the Runner's direction. "And I cannot tell you more than I told him."

"Where was Halsey's trainer on the night The Miller was poisoned?" Mad Jack demanded.

"Sim went with the others to have his dinner, as they always do."

"And drink themselves into oblivion, I suppose?"

"A pint of ale never did any man harm, sir."

"Leaving you alone to guard the stables?"

Old Peter glanced in the Runner's direction. Theo Bryght was silent. He had as little desire to further involve Sam in this sorry affair as Old Peter.

"You must have seen something, or heard something," Mad Jack persisted. "Perhaps you saw William Halsey enter the stables. That would be a natural thing to see. Perhaps Mr. Halsey wished to say something to Sim, give some instruction."

The Runner wondered if Mad Jack was having second thoughts about who killed The Miller of Dee, or if he was merely seeking confirmation, before he stormed the Castle and throttled the young man with his bare hands, thereby cheating the law of putting a noose around Halsey's neck.

Meanwhile, Old Peter was calmly shaking his head, seemingly oblivious to the storm brewing beside him.

"Old man," said Mad Jack, "hemlock could not have gotten mixed with the hay of its own accord."

"No, sir, I suppose it could not."

Mad Jack made a movement to raise his whip, but Theo Bryght just as quickly laid a warning hand on his arm.

"What happened to Halsey's trainer, Old Peter?" asked the Runner. "Is he still in Chester?"

"Mr. Halsey dismissed him the next morning. I believe Sim took the mail coach to London."

"Simmons would not have had anything to do with this," said Mad Jack, striking the ground with his whip. "He has worked for me. He has a tendency to press too hard when he smells a winner, but that is the worst that can be said for him."

"Men have been tempted by money before," said Theo Bryght. "If someone hired him to be an accomplice, or bought his silence —"

"Simmons would have fled rather than harm a horse under his care. If word got out, his career would be over."

"If you gentlemen have no more need of me," said Old Peter, "I shall get back to my work."

Old Peter ambled off in the direction of the stable. When the stable hand was some distance away Theo Bryght called out, "Old Peter!" The elderly man turned. The Runner threw a coin, which was duly caught.

"At least we know Old Peter is not deaf," said Bryght.

"No, his ears are sharp enough. He would have heard if someone had been sneaking around the stable, all right. If Halsey paid off anyone, it was that one."

The Runner silently agreed. And he wondered how he could gain Old Peter's trust, for surely the man knew more than he had revealed so far.

"If Halsey poisoned The Miller, he is the biggest fool in the world," Mad Jack added, giving the ground another blow with his whip. "Cavalier is a fine horse for show, but he has not got the temperament to be a first class race horse. The Miller would have beaten Cavalier to the finish line any day of the week. Anyone could have seen that."

"But if the young man had creditors —"

"He should have told them to wait until the spring, until the racing season began. They would have gotten their money and Halsey still would have had his horse. That is what any sensible man would have done."

Theo Bryght was tempted to laugh. If there was one person who was eminently not sensible — who was entirely guided by his overwrought emotions — it was Mad Jack Mytton. But in Mad Jack, unlike Halsey, those emotions worked in his favor, adding to the forcefulness of his already striking personality; it would be easy to imagine him metaphorically whipping his creditors into obedience — and using a real whip should words and threats not accomplish the task. And so the Runner said, "Perhaps Mr. Halsey does not have the temperament for the racecourse."

"Too impatient, you mean?"

Theo Bryght looked around the green expanse. The openness of the place — the lack of secret hiding places, the outward lack of a potential for mystery — seemed to mock him. But then he had a moment when the fog began to lift. There were many keys when it came to unlocking the human puzzle that lay at the core of any crime, and his instincts told him Mad Jack had just handed him one he needed. "Yes, perhaps that is what I mean."

Ella had not worked as a parlor maid for several years, not since becoming the personal maid of Lady Ashe. But she had not forgotten how to lay a fire or polish the brass, and the Steele house, although large by Chester's standards, was much smaller than Hopewell, the Yorkshire home of Lady Ashe. The young woman was also not one to put on airs, and so when Milly, the personal maid of Mary and Emily Steele, packed her small trunk and left, Ella added the duties of a lady's maid to her other chores. Thus, she was able to go freely throughout the house, and by the end of her first day of work her presence was hardly noted at all.

After Mr. Thomas Steele had been transported to his final resting place, with much dignity and solemnity, there was only one last task to attend to before this chapter in the family's history could be considered complete: the reading of the will. The family solicitor, Mr. Myrditch, was therefore summoned, the family members were gathered in the drawing room, and Ella found much polishing work to busy herself with in the adjoining room, whose connecting door had been left slightly ajar.

Mr. Myrditch, a man who was as sober in dress as he was in temperament, was not a man for small talk. After offering his condolences and polishing his already sparkling clean spectacles, he removed the will from his coat pocket and proceeded to read it through.

The bulk of the estate—the house, the silk business, the other pieces of property located in the Rows, the bulk of the money invested in the Consols, as well as the race horse Cavalier — all went to Mr. Alexander Steele, the deceased's son. The daughters of the deceased, Miss Mary and Miss Emily Steele, were each to receive a gift of £2500, also invested in the Consols. A few small bequests had been bestowed upon some long-time, loyal employees of the silk mercer's business establishment, as well as a few of the servants. It was all quite usual, Mr. Myrditch assured the family, except in one thing.

"Should Mr. Alexander Steele die without children," the solicitor intoned, "the estate will pass to the eldest surviving daughter. The wife of Mr. Alexander Steele, should there be a surviving widow, shall receive a one-time gift of £5,000."

Mr. Myrditch, having discharged his duty, refused an offer to stay for tea and left.

The family sat in silence for several minutes. The contents of the will had not been totally unexpected; the daughters knew the son would inherit most of their father's fortune. Yet, in truth, they had not expected their own portion to be so small. Emily did not have a head for complex mathematics but figuring the income from the funds — which yielded five percent — was something practically any girl could do. From being young ladies of fortune, she and her sister had become ladies with only £125 annum apiece, practically paupers.

"Oh, Mary," she murmured. Her sister's icy glance silenced her. Yet she was not offended. She knew Mary hated hysterical scenes in public. They would discuss what to do later, behind closed doors.

Mary stood up and removed the housekeeping keys from the pouch that hung from her dress. Handing them to Julia, she said, "I hope you will be happy here, ma'am."

Alexander snatched the keys away before they fell to the floor; Julia was too stunned to take them.

"Really, Mary, there is no need to be so tragic," said Alexander. "You must continue to run things here, at least until you and Emily will have decided what you want to do."

"Yes, this is still your home, Miss Steele," said Julia.

"No, ma'am, it is not. We have all heard the terms of the will. My sister and I are now your guests. I hope we shall not cause you undue inconvenience."

Mary left the room, her head held high, taking with her an invisible cloak of chilly air.

Emily was unsure if she should follow her sister or stay. Everything was so upside down. She had known there would be changes, after her father died, but she had never thought seriously about how those changes would affect her situation. Or, to put it more honestly, she had assumed she would be happily married and with a home of her own when that sad event occurred.

Her thoughts flew to William Halsey — and sank, like a bird downed by a hunter's gun. They had never discussed money, of course. Talk of such matters would have been out of place on the dance floor or the promenade around the Walls. But she knew that in addition to his admiration for her there were certain expectations. Her father's wealth was no secret in Chester. It would have been assumed her father would provide for her generously. She also knew that if she could bring only £125 annum to the marriage, there was no hope for them — even if Halsey was deemed innocent when his case was tried.

"I think we all need some tea," Alexander was saying.

Emily, feeling the tears welling up in her eyes, whispered, "I am sorry, I have such a headache," and rushed out of the room.

Two pairs of eyes followed her. Two pairs of ears waited until they heard the sound of her footsteps race up the stairs.

"Well, Mrs. Steele," said Alexander, handing the keys to his wife. "Here are the keys to our new life."

CHAPTER XI
ELLA TAKES A TUMBLE

THEO BRYGHT STROLLED DOWN the center of Chester, with a new guide to the city in his hand. "Look interested, Lauferby," he said under his breath to his companion. Then, resuming his normal tone of voice, he continued, "This part was written by Robinson Crusoe himself, old Daniel Defoe."

"It wearies me enough when these fellows write a story," Lauferby complained, "I cannot think why a person should bother to write about a town."

"Well, he did, and this is what he has to say. 'Nor do the Rows, as they call them, add anything, in my opinion, to the beauty of the city, but just the contrary, they serve to make the city look both old and ugly …'"

"I would agree with that," said Lauferby, casting a dismal look about the place. "Really, whatever could the builders have been thinking? What purpose do these dark and dreary galleries serve?"

"Perhaps Mr. Defoe will tell us. He continues, 'These Rows are certain long galleries, up one pair of stairs, which run along the side of the streets, before all the houses, tho' joined to them, and as is pretended, they are to keep the people dry in walking along. This they do effectually, but then they take away all the view of the houses from the street, nor can a stranger, that was to ride thro' Chester, see any shops in the city; besides, they make the shops themselves dark, and the way in them is dark, dirty, and uneven.'"

Theo Bryght stopped, causing Lord Lauferby to stop as well. They had been walking up Watergate Street and now they had reached the point where the four Rows met. Trying not to draw attention, the Runner studied the Bridge Street Row in particular, shifting his eyes from his book to the actual Row.

"There is a steep staircase," he said nodding toward the stone steps cut into the wall. "There is the covered walkway, joined to the houses on the second floor, one of which belongs to the Steele family. Yes, the gallery would protect passersby from the rain. On the other side of the street, though, there appear to be shops on the second floor, as well as the first. I wonder where the mercer's shop is ... ah, there it is.   Thomas Steele, Mercer and Milliner. It does not look dark, but then the entrance is on the first floor, accessible from the street, and not from the Row above. Chester has changed since Mr. Defoe visited it a century ago."

"What shall we do now, Bryght?"

"I should like to have a look inside."

"Go inside a silk mercer's shop? Have you taken leave of your senses?"

"Would you not like to surprise your mother with silk for a new dress?"

"My mother would be appalled by the impudence. Choosing silks is a woman's business."

Their talk was interrupted by a great clamor of hoof beats, a roar of voices, and a sudden whooshing noise. Mr. Bryght looked up.

"Lauferby, was that a horse that just flew over our heads?"

"Yes, I think it was."

A great rush of men flew into the street, following the horse, which had landed on the Row opposite. The rider barely missed having his head cut off by the overhang of the Row's low ceiling.

A moment later, the rider returned and led the horse down the steep stairs, to the cheers of the crowd. Taking off his hat and waving it in the air, Mad Jack Mytton shouted to the crowd, "Well, men, have I fulfilled my part of the bargain or not? Did I jump this horse from one side of Bridge Street Row to the other or not?"

The crowd cheered.

"Who will you vote for?"

"Lord Grosvenor!"

"I did not hear you!"

"Lord Grosvenor!"

"We must conclude this bargain over a pint of ale. Follow me!"

Mad Jack galloped down the street, followed by the crowd, who were still shouting "Lord Grosvenor!" as they ran.

Theo Bryght looked after them. "They tell me that in some parts of the world a political election is considered to be as serious a business as choosing a silk for a new dress. If you will not go with me to the mercer's shop, Lauferby, pay a visit to the tobacconist across the way."

"Very well. What should I ask?"

"Try to find out what you can about Thomas Steele — if he was well liked, if he was the sort to hold a grudge, what blend of tobacco he preferred."

"Are you serious?"

"One never knows for certain what will inspire a person to talk, Lauferby, but I would say it was a safe bet to assume a discussion about tobacco would interest an owner of a tobacco shop."

The two parted. Theo Bryght approached the silk mercer's shop. A glance inside the place almost made him lose his courage. The shop was much larger than it appeared from the street, and throughout the cavernous

space shop assistants simpered and pranced, bringing
bolts of cloth to the waiting ladies like acolytes must have
brought offerings to the temple of Venus in days of yore.
A black-haired youth stood at the shop's door, bowing
and smirking as he handed ladies into their waiting
carriages. He looked at the Runner inquisitively, but with
the obsequious politeness that so often came with men in
trade.

"I would like to speak with the proprietor," said the
Runner.

"Mr. Steele died, sir, last week."

"Is there a manager?"

"Certainly, sir. Who should I say wishes to speak
with Mr. Tilson?"

"Theo Bryght, Bow Street Runner."

Mr. Tilson, who had overheard the conversation,
turned his attention away from a cascade of brocades,
and came at once to usher the Runner into his private
chamber. Behind the smiling façade lay a shrewd
intelligence, the Runner guessed; otherwise, Thomas
Steele would not have continued to employ him.

"I shall not waste your time, Mr. Tilson. I would like
to know about Mr. Thomas Steele."

"What would you like to know, sir?" asked the
manager, removing a large handkerchief from a pocket to
wipe his slightly red nose

"For one, did he have any enemies?"

"Not that I know of, sir. Of course, Thomas Steele
was a shrewd businessman. I will not say he was not —
and some might say he was a hard man, when it came to
his business. Yet he could be generous, as well."

"In what way was he a hard man?"

"He would buy the shops of his competitors."

"Mr. Steele did not like competition?"

"Most tradesmen do not."

"Could one assume, then, that these other merchants were not overly fond of Mr. Steele?"

"They received a fair price. As I said, Mr. Steele could be generous. He did not wish to ruin the men, you understand. He simply preferred that they conduct their business elsewhere."

"So they left Chester?"

"Or turned their hands to other things."

"In your opinion, then, there was no shopkeeper in Chester who hated Mr. Steele enough to kill him?"

"Chester is a market town, Mr. Bryght. Commerce is in our blood. If a person cannot sell hats, he will sell ale. If he cannot sell ale, he will sell tooth powder. He will do what he can to succeed, which rarely includes holding on to a grudge."

"Did Mr. Steele's distaste for competition extend to the racecourse?"

"I was not privy to his private affairs."

"What will happen to the shop now?"

For the first time during the interview Mr. Tilson dropped his mask, and a wistful look appeared upon his face as he gave his nose another wipe. "I do not know, sir. That is for the family to decide."

"Will Thomas Steele be missed, do you think, Mr. Tilson?"

"Missed?" The shop manager was clearly taken by surprise.

"I do not mean by his family, who will surely feel the absence of their father. I was referring to Chester. Did Mr. Steele make a contribution to the town?"

"He was active in Chester politics. He was one of the Independents. But ..."

Mr. Tilson slid open a panel in the wall, through which he had a view of the activity taking place on the shop floor — the ladies dressed in their smart hats and elegant gowns, the assistants unfurling their bolts of silk and muslin.

"Life will continue?" the Runner suggested.

"Yes, life will continue. Of course, Thomas Steele was a personality, a forceful man, who made his mark on this town. But will anyone miss him, or any of us, in fifty years? That I cannot say. And I cannot say most people would want the actual facts of their lives to be remembered — their thoughts, their—"

The manager slid the panel back into place with a sharp snap.

When Bryght returned to the street, he was still puzzled by the philosophical bent of Tilson's final remarks. Not that a shop manager had to be preoccupied day and night by the price of muslin and the latest fashion in trims, but there was a wistfulness, a sense of regret, about the manager that Bryght had not expected to find. But since it was not the manager he was interested in, he pushed his thoughts aside and hailed Lord Lauferby, who was just making his exit from the tobacconist's shop.

"What did our tobacco seller have to say?"

"He did not like our Mr. Steele."

"Indeed?"

"He said Mr. Steele thought he owned Bridge Street and could tell the other shop owners what to do."

"He was not sorry to see Mr. Steele dead, then?"

"He did not say that. On the contrary, he was shocked to hear Mr. Steele had been poisoned. One can dislike a person, Bryght, but not necessarily wish to see this person dead."

"True. Well, let us go and see what some other of our Chester merchants have to say."

When Ella brought up the requested cup of tea, she could see that Emily had been crying. The young Miss Steele quickly brushed away her tears and directed the maid to put the tea on a table.

"I tore the hem of my dress. Do you know how to repair it?"

"Yes, Miss."

"I have forgotten your name."

"Ella, Miss. Shall I help you into another frock, Miss, so this torn one can be repaired right away?"

"Yes. It is one of my favorite gowns."

Emily fought back the tears. If it was a favorite gown, it was because William Halsey had always made a point of telling her how well she looked when she wore it.

When Ella had finished doing up the buttons of the new frock, she took the torn one with her down to the servants' quarters. The cook was preparing the family's dinner, and a delicious aroma filled the room. Margaret was doing some sewing and trying her best to hide the fact that her eyes drifted to the cook after every few stitches. It was not that the servant girl truly suspected the cook of being a crazed poisoner, but that was how things stood at the Steele home; everyone wanted to believe the others were innocent, without quite succeeding.

Ella joined Margaret by the fire and began to do her own sewing. For several minutes they worked in silence, and Ella, for one, enjoyed the opportunity to sit before the warm fire and do some quiet work. But the peaceful scene came to an end when Margaret suddenly looked up from her mending and whispered, "What was that?"

Ella put down her needle and listened. "I didn't hear anything, except for Cook chopping the vegetables."

"Oh."

They went back to their work. A few minutes later the quiet was again disturbed, this time by the sound of a large crash. Margaret jumped up from her stool as though it had caught on fire and ran over to where the cook was working.

"It's the murderer!" she gasped.

"Nonsense," replied the older woman. "They have arrested the murderer."

"Someone is in the cellar," the girl insisted.

"Probably a cat," said the cook. "They're always knocking over something."

"Yes, it was probably a cat," said Ella, trying to reassure the other girl. She then turned to the cook and said, "Shouldn't someone see what got knocked over? You wouldn't want animals to get into your storage bins."

The cook looked at the door that led down to the cellar without enthusiasm.

"Give me a candle and I'll do it," said Ella.

"Oh, no, Ella! You mustn't!" Margaret cried out.

"We are agreed it is a cat, are we not?" Ella replied, taking the candle from the cook.

The cook opened the door for her, and Ella descended down a steep flight of stairs. The air grew progressively damper and colder. She was not exactly afraid, but she did come to the conclusion that it was much easier to be brave when in a warm and well-lit room than when in an underground vault that was dark and damp. When her foot sank into a freezing puddle, her spirits sank with it.

Yet a voice within her assured her there was really nothing to be afraid of. Even if the murderer had been wandering in the cellar, the loud crash would have sent him running. She therefore proceeded with her search, taking care to shield her candle's flame from the drafts.

Presently she came upon an overturned barrel. She surmised it was this that had caused the noise. Fortunately, the barrel's lid was still tightly fastened and so none of the contents had spilled out. A little further on she saw a small window that was cut into the wall and admitted a tiny square of sunlight.

It was surprising that the window was not barred or secured in any way. Perhaps the pane of glass had been broken and the family had forgotten to fix it. Or perhaps it had been left unsecured on purpose. And so she continued toward the window like a plant that reaches upward toward the light, neither looking around her or beneath her.

Which is why, when she stumbled and fell, she was so surprised she let out a loud and piercing scream.

Her candle was extinguished by the fall, but there was just enough light pouring in through the window for her to see a small, dark figure dart through the bins and barrels and jump up to the opening. In a moment it was gone.

Ella ran after it, but she was too large to squeeze her way through the gap in the wall. All she could do was peer at the view outside, which seemed to be some sort of back alleyway.

Her cry had apparently been heard by the rest of the house, for soon afterward she heard loud wails — which she assumed were coming from Margaret — and the sounds of hurried footsteps overhead. A moment later she heard footsteps coming down the stairs and she could see the dim flames of several candles.

"Ella!" a man's voice called out.

"Ella!" called out a second voice, which she recognized as belonging to the cook.

"I'm over here, by the window," Ella called out in reply.

As the group drew closer, Ella recognized her rescuers. Mr. Alexander Steele led the search party, which also consisted of the cook and Mary Steele.

"Whatever it was, it escaped through there," she explained, pointing to the window. She then added, "It could not have been a cat. It was much too large."

"Could you not see what it was?" Miss Steele asked impatiently.

"No, ma'am. It was dark and it all happened so quickly. I was taken by surprise."

"Can you not make a guess?" asked Mr. Steele.

Ella thought for a moment. "If I were to call it anything, I suppose … I suppose I should call it a child."

"A child?" the cook asked with surprise. "What should a child be doing in our cellar?"

"Perhaps it was hungry."

"You should see to the window, Mr. Steele," said Mary. "It is dangerous to leave an opening to the house unsecured."

Mary turned and made her way back to the stairs.

"Thank goodness no harm was done," Alexander said to the others. "That is, you are not hurt, are you, Ella?"

"No, sir,"

"Cook, please see to having that window repaired right away. We do not — "

An exclamation of surprise from Mary Steele's lips stopped him in mid-sentence. They all rushed to her.

"What is it?" asked Mr. Steele.

Mary showed him a sealed packet that she held in her hand. "I do not know, Mr. Steele. But I intend to find out."

CHAPTER XII
A PATTERN EMERGES

THEO BRYGHT WAS EXACTLY where he wished to be — sitting in the drawing room of No. 10 Bridge Street Row. He was careful not to signal in any way to the parlor maid serving round the tea — he would converse with Ella in private later — but, instead, kept his attention focused on the woman who was speaking.

"I had no wish to invite the law into this house before, Mr. Bryght," Mary Steele was saying. "But this matter has gone too far."

"What exactly did you find in the cellar, Miss Steele?"

"This," said the lady, handing over the still-sealed packet to the Runner.

Theo Bryght turned the packet over in his hand. It appeared to have come from an apothecary's shop.

"I insist Mr. Willows be sent for, and that he examine the contents of this packet in front of us all," Mary continued. "His apothecary shop is just a few doors down."

Bryght had no objection, and the man was summoned. While they waited the Runner took the opportunity to visit the room that had belonged to Mr. Thomas Steele, accompanied by the son. The room had been cleaned and aired, and so there was nothing left to see of Mr. Steele's gruesome final hours, but the sight helped the Runner to better visualize the sequence of events that had occurred on the fatal afternoon.

The Runner went over to the window and looked down to the alleyway below. "This is the way the stable boy entered, is it not?"

"Yes. His entry took me very much by surprise," Alexander replied.

"Have you seen him since?"

"No, though I am not sure if I would recognize him if I did. It was a horrid day."

"I am sure it was. Your sisters must find it comforting that you are here."

A bitter smile appeared on the young man's face. "Have you heard about the will, Mr. Bryght?"

"No."

"I will save you a visit to the family solicitor, or the Black Lion. I inherit everything, except for a few trifling bequests to my father's servants and workers at the shop and a ridiculously small sum of money to my two sisters. Mrs. Steele and I are discussing how we can remedy this unfortunate situation and rectify the injustice that has been done to the Miss Steeles. But for the present, I should not think my presence here in this house is much of a comfort. Indeed, I should not be surprised if at least one of my sisters wished I were dead."

"How can you say that, Alexander?"

The two men turned. Emily Steele was standing in the doorway.

"Is it not enough that Father has died so horridly?" the girl pleaded. "Must you and Mary speak so despicably about one another, too? I cannot stand it any longer. I cannot!"

Alexander rushed over to his sister. "Emily, please. I am sorry. I was not thinking. I am sure Mr. Bryght will forget what I have just said. Is that not so, Mr. Bryght?"

Theo Bryght gave a slight bow, which he allowed the brother and sister to interpret as they pleased.

"Mr. Willows has arrived," said Emily, having regained her composure somewhat.

While the two men followed her back to the drawing room, Bryght stopped and said, "I have forgotten my hat. Miss Steele, could I trouble you to escort me back to your father's room?"

"A servant can fetch it for you," said Alexander.

"I do not mind, Alexander."

Mr. Steele continued down the stairs. When the Runner was alone with Emily, he asked, "Did you receive a letter from William Halsey on the day your father died?"

"No."

"Miss Steele, if you did, I beg of you to speak the truth. Your lover's life may depend upon it."

"I would give my own life to save his, but I received no letter."

"When you did receive a letter from him, how was it delivered? Was Sam your courier?"

"Sam is a good child."

"I know he is. But was he your messenger?"

"Yes. He often visited father. During the visit he would place William's letter behind the mirror or retrieve one I had placed there for Mr. Halsey. I would take the letter when I was alone with Father."

"Did anyone else know of this arrangement?"

"I do not think so."

"Not even Mrs. Watson?"

"If she knew, she did not read the letters. The seal was never broken."

"Have you looked behind the mirror since your father died?

In reply, Emily rushed to the bureau and reached her hand behind the mirror that sat above it. The disappointed expression on her face told the Runner that she had not found any letter.

Mr. Willows was shown into the drawing room after Bryght and Emily joined the family. The apothecary was a nondescript fellow, Bryght noted, with what some might consider a calming demeanor. Bryght personally did not care for the way the man practically tip-toed into the room, but he supposed such caution may have been the result of spending much time among the sick.

Mr. Willows gingerly opened the packet. After smelling the contents and examining a few grains in his hand, he placed one of those grains on his tongue.

"A slightly acrid taste," he murmured, more to himself than to the others, "and a tingling sensation on the tongue and lips. Yes, it could be."

"It could be what?" asked Alexander Steele. Julia slipped her hand into his.

Mr. Willows, who had been lost in thought, returned his attention to the group. "Aconite. Or Monkshead, if you like that name better. Highly poisonous. It has its medicinal uses, of course, but it is definitely not the sort of thing that should be left lying about."

"Was this what killed Mr. Thomas Steele?" asked the Runner.

"I cannot be absolutely sure, but it is very possible. It would cause the symptoms Mr. Carlstone described at the inquest."

"You mentioned that this drug has medicinal purposes. Did Mr. Thomas Steele ever take Aconite for his ailments?"

"I cannot say he never used it. Aconite is sometimes given when there is a high fever or congestion in the lungs. But I do not recall being asked to prepare a packet for anyone in this house, at least not recently. And I should never have given such a large quantity."

"Would you know if this packet came from your shop, Mr. Willows?"

"I am afraid not, Mr. Bryght. As you can see, the packet has no markings. And it is the type of packet commonly used by people in my trade. I do not see how one would know where this particular preparation came from."

Mr. Willows was allowed to tip-toe out of the room and return to his place of business. Mr. Bryght was shown the cellar, where the packet was found, as well as the alleyway that stood in back of the house.

"It is a busy place," he commented.

"Carters unload the merchandise here and carry it across the street to the shop," explained Mary Steele. "We allow other merchants to use the area, as well."

"At night, though, I suppose this back street is quiet."

"My father was killed during the day."

Mr. Bryght wondered why Mary Steele made no effort to be soft and appealing. She surely guessed she was under suspicion, as was everyone in the house, despite the arrest of William Halsey. Yet she had not made a single attempt to win his sympathy.

"Do you intend to remain in the house, Miss Steele?"

"That is entirely up to my brother and Mrs. Steele."

"I thought you might wish to find lodgings elsewhere of your own accord."

"Why do you think that?"

"Well, if the murderer is still about, you might be in danger. Or are you satisfied with the jury's verdict?"

"The jury was comprised of idiots, Mr. Bryght. You know that, as well as I do. But why should I be in danger? I inherited only £2500."

"People have killed for less."

"Someone murdered my father. I intend to find out who it was. I shall not be scared away, Mr. Bryght."

The puzzle of Miss Mary Steele took Theo Bryght all the way to Stanley Hall, where he and Lauferby had been invited to dinner. A servant led them to the back of the house, to a spacious library that gave way to a terrace which, in turn, gave way to one of those magical scenes so common to English country life, the perfectly landscaped lawn and garden. It was a gracious scene, made even more glorious by the reddish-golden glow cast by the last rays of sunshine. In such a setting it was almost possible to think that such things as murder and jealousy and hate could not exist.

But if that were true, he would not exist, either. For he felt a pang of jealousy as he watched Sir Richard Halsey escort Lady Ashe around the ornamental lake. He did not ascribe unsuitable motives to Sir Richard, who he knew had lent his arm solely in his role as affable host. It was the easiness, the naturalness that the Runner envied. It was a pretty world, but when he was invited to enter this world it was not to add to its beauty. His role was to shatter the illusion, to discover the rot and decay lurking within.

His presence was discovered, and the group came toward him and Lauferby. At the head were Lady Halsey and Mrs. Seymour, followed by Lady Ashe and Sir Richard. They did not discuss the business that had brought the Runner to Chester over dinner, partly because the dinner was too good to spoil with such unpleasantness and partly because one did not discuss personal matters in front of the servants, whom Sir

Richard and his lady kept busy, despite the smallness of the party. It was only after the men had rejoined the ladies in the drawing room that the topic that was foremost on all their minds could be spoken of.

"And you may speak freely in front of Lady Ashe and Mrs. Seymour," Sir Richard said to the Runner. "Lady Ashe is practically a member of the family."

"Have you any news for us, Mr. Bryght?" asked Lady Halsey, fixing her striking green eyes upon the Runner.

"Unfortunately, my lady, an investigation of this nature takes time."

"For the life of me, I cannot understand why that jury thought my son poisoned Thomas Steele," said Sir Richard. "And please do not bring up his unfortunate infatuation with the Steele girl. If every thwarted lover murdered his young lady's parents, there would be no elders in England."

"I hope you will pardon my impudence for asking this, Sir Richard," said Bryght, "but is there any reason why the merchants of Chester might hold a grudge against you or members of your family?"

Lady Halsey exchanged glances with her husband. "I can think of no reason," said Sir Richard. "William owed money to a few shopkeepers, or so I have been told. But such things happen all the time."

"There is nothing else?"

The mask of jovial county squire dropped from Sir Richard's face, and his features turned hard as he affixed his gaze upon the Bow Street Runner. "Are you toying with me, Mr. Bryght? If you have spent any time in a Chester alehouse it is impossible you do not already know."

"I spent today at the Roodee and at the home of the Steeles."

"It is nothing but an attempt at revenge," said Lady Halsey. "It is Mr. Talbot who should be sitting in jail, and not my son."

"Talbot is the merchant who spoke against our son at the inquest," Sir Richard explained.

"He has a grudge against your son?"

"Not against William — at least William is not the cause of the grudge. The trouble concerned our eldest son, George." This time, Sir Richard glanced in the direction of Lady Ashe, before saying, "But I do not think this is a topic that should be discussed in front of the ladies."

"I am not a Miss from the schoolroom," Charlotte assured him. "Neither is my aunt."

"Very well then, I shall speak candidly," said Sir Richard. "Talbot's daughter caught the eye of my son, George. She was a pretty girl."

"She threw herself in his way," said Lady Halsey. "Then she tried to force George to marry her."

"Such a marriage was impossible, of course," Sir Richard continued. "We offered to give the family money, so the girl could go elsewhere to have her child. Instead, she threw herself into the river and drowned. We have sent George to the Continent for a few months. It seemed the talk and hard feelings were finally starting to die down. But now Talbot has found his opportunity to take his revenge on our family. I only wish I were sitting in that jail, and not William. It is not fair that he should take the blame for what his brother has done."

Theo Bryght studiously kept his gaze on a porcelain figurine sitting on the mantelpiece as he said, "I assume William Halsey's intentions toward Miss Steele are more honorable."

A sharp intake of breath coming from the direction of Lady Halsey assured him his remark had caused offense, but there had been no way to avoid it; the question had to be asked.

"He mentioned that he wished to marry the young woman."

"Are you against the marriage, Sir Richard?"

"I cannot truthfully say I am pleased by the idea."

"But you would allow them to marry?"

Sir Richard paused before saying, "I would have continued to try to prevent it. It is not a suitable match for my son."

"Even though Thomas Steele was very wealthy?"

"Wealth is not everything, Mr. Bryght," said Lady Halsey.

"Very true, my lady. But I understand Mr. William Halsey has more debts than prospects."

"That is not entirely true," said Sir Richard. "Lady Halsey and I have hopes for arranging a marriage between William and the daughter of a local squire who possesses a fine estate. We are certain his infatuation with Miss Steele will pass, with time. These things usually do."

Theo Bryght caught a glimpse of Lady Ashe's reflection in a mirror. Her expression was calm, almost blank, and he wondered if this talk about money and marriage was causing her distress, reminding her of her own unhappy marriage to Lord Ashe. He hoped she was made of sterner stuff; otherwise his own hopes for the future were doomed.

But he was not in Chester for his own purposes, and so he returned his attention to Sir Richard and asked, "What were your own relations with Thomas Steele?"

"My relations?"

"Did you ever quarrel?"

Sir Richard hesitated for a moment. "I hardly knew the man. I am not active in Chester affairs."

"Could you have once insulted Mr. Steele, even unintentionally?"

"Why should I do that?"

"I understand Mr. Steele bought up a sizeable amount of property in Chester," said Bryght. "If he could do that and fund a political party, he must have been quite a wealthy man. And sometimes newly wealthy men forget their true position in society."

"It is true he tried to play the lord of the manor, but it was ludicrous of Steele to think he could buy up more property in the Rows than Lord Grosvenor."

"It was not then only a business decision, to prevent competition? Local politics were also a factor?"

"It comes to the same thing. When the Grosvenors buy a building, they lease the shops and houses at favorable terms to their supporters. Steele tried to do the same for the Independents' followers, on a much smaller scale, of course. He was wealthy for a silk mercer, but his wealth could not compare with the Grosvenor fortune."

"Sir Richard, I continue to be puzzled by one thing. Why was Thomas Steele so adamantly opposed to his daughter marrying your son? If, as you say, there was no quarrel between the two of you, I should think he would be pleased to have his daughter marry into the gentry."

It was Lady Halsey who replied. "That is because you never met him. He was a proud man, Mr. Bryght. He would not have wanted to feel inferior to his son-in-law's family. He would not have wanted to feel inferior to anyone."

The clock struck nine when the door to Charlotte's sitting room opened and Ella walked in. Ella glanced at the assembled company and said, "I am sorry to keep you waiting, my lady."

"Have you had your supper, Ella?"

"Yes, my lady. I ate with the servants at the Steele home."

Ella quickly took off her bonnet and smoothed down her hair, which was already perfectly neat.

"Lady Ashe, would you mind if Ella sits during our interview?" asked Theo Bryght, who had come to Charlotte's inn with Lord Lauferby to learn what Ella had discovered during her sojourn at the Steele home. Sir Richard had also come with them, to the Runner's private dismay; he preferred there to be as few people in the room as possible when he conducted his inquiries, and this one was turning into yet another social gathering. But since Sir Richard was paying his fee, the Runner had not felt he could say no — and so they were all in the sitting room, waiting to hear what Ella had learned.

"She has most likely had a long and tiresome day," Bryght added, "and my questions may take some time."

Ella, however, quickly assured the group that she was not the least bit tired. The Runner inwardly smiled. An English servant—or at least the ones who took real pride in their work — were a pleasant mystery to him. For someone like Ella, it would be easier to sit on hot coals than sit in a drawing room while in the presence of her lady.

"As you please, Ella, and have you anything to tell us?"

"I noticed several things, Mr. Bryght. Shall I begin with the reading of the will, or the suspicions of the servants, or the incident in the cellar?"

"The will," he said, noting that both Sir Richard and Lord Lauferby were sitting in their chairs a little straighter.

"The bulk of the estate goes to the son, Mr. Alexander Steele," said Ella.

"I assume that was expected," said the Runner. "But what of the daughters, how have they been provided for?"

"The Miss Steeles are to receive £2500 each, invested in the Consols."

"The old fool!" Lauferby blurted out. "Is there another father so cruel?!"

"Not cruel, and not a fool," said Sir Richard. "Most likely, Mr. Steele wanted to protect his daughters from fortune hunters. That is something responsible fathers do."

"Surely. Sir Richard, you are not accusing your own son of being a fortune hunter," said Lord Lauferby.

"I am a realist, sir. A gentleman with no fortune of his own must seek it elsewhere. And I will not pretend I am not pleased by this turn of events. I felt from the beginning my son would not be happy with a tradesman's daughter. This new information confirms it."

"Perhaps we can move on to the cellar," said Lady Ashe.

"By all means," said Bryght, who was beginning to develop a dislike for Sir Richard, who had perhaps forgotten that Lady Ashe's family had its roots in commerce and trade. The Runner wondered if he would ever stop unintentionally hurting Charlotte, or if his profession would always be the source of painful reminders from the past.

Ella recounted her story. Although Bryght had already heard most of the details from Mary Steele, this was his first opportunity to question Ella directly, and so he asked, "You are sure it was a child?"

"I cannot say I would swear on the Bible," Ella replied, "but it seemed to me to be someone quite small."

"And you did not see its face, or recognize the clothing?"

"No, the cellar was dimly lit and it all happened so quickly I had no time to gain more than a fleeting impression."

"Do you think it was Sam?" Charlotte asked the Runner.

"It could have been," said Bryght, "especially if he was hungry and searching for food. But in truth it could have been any child. I would suppose the vaults underneath the Rows are irresistible to children. An open window would make it doubly so."

"Why would Sam be hiding in the vaults?" asked Sir Richard.

"He is missing. Have you not heard?"

"No. Why should he be missing?"

"Because of something he might have seen, of course," said Lord Lauferby.

Theo Bryght would have liked to kick his companion, but he did not have the heart to dirty the young lord's spotless cream-colored pantaloons.

Sir Richard was looking bewildered. "Seen? At the stable?"

"Or at the Steele home," said Bryght, before Lauferby could say more.

"When the boy gets hungry enough, he will return to the stable," said Sir Richard, regaining his composure.

"Although I very much doubt he would have anything of value to say about what happened to The Miller."

"Why do you say that, Sir Richard?" asked the Runner.

"Sam is a bright lad, where horses are concerned. But he lets his imagination run away from him. I remember the time he swore he saw the ghost of a Cavalier sitting in Pemberton's Parlour. The child insisted he heard the ghost calling for a tankard of mulled wine and some bread and cheese."

"I should think every child of Chester must see a Cavalier's ghost at least once in his or her life," said Lady Ashe. "The Walls are so full of history — and romance."

Theo Bryght hoped it was not his imagination that was running wild at that moment, and that Lady Ashe had really glanced at him when she spoke that final word.

"You are quite right, my dear," said Mrs. Seymour, who, as usual, had not missed a thing. "Even if Sam did say he saw a ghost, in a place like Chester it would be quite natural."

Sir Richard, who did not like to be contradicted, testily replied, "To see a ghost is one thing, Mrs. Seymour. To say you have heard a ghost order his supper is an embellishment that suggests a too active imagination."

Before an altercation could occur, the Runner asked if Ella had anything more to report. She did, and she proceeded to describe the finding of the packet of poison by Mary Steele, which further fueled the suspicions of some members of the household, as well as the servants, that a murderer was in their midst.

"One can excuse such fiddle-faddle in a servant," said Sir Richard, "but I am surprised at Mrs. Steele. She must be a very weak-spirited creature to believe one of the Miss Steeles is out to poison her."

"I think we must make allowances for Mrs. Steele," said Lady Ashe. "She is a total stranger in these parts and most likely still fatigued from her journey. The strain of the past several days would try the good judgment of most people."

"And do not forget that she is from Italy," said Lord Lauferby. "I hear they poison people quite often in that part of the world."

CHAPTER XIII
THE PIECES ARE RE-ARRANGED

AFTER THE OTHERS HAD LEFT and Mrs. Seymour and Ella had retired to their rooms, Charlotte took a seat beside the hearth, where a fire was still smoldering. She wished she knew if Ella's sojourn in the Steele household had been deemed a success by Theo Bryght. He had not divulged his own thoughts on the matter. There was no reason why he should. Yet as Charlotte watched the remains of the fire give off their last warming glow, she thought it would be nice to sit with him before some comfortable hearth of their own, talking over the day's events, before retiring for the night.

She did not let her thoughts go further than that. What would happen behind the bed curtains was not what stopped her from dropping the veneer of reserve she still preserved while in his presence. If only she could be sure she would not mind saying goodbye forever to "Lady Ashe," would not miss the condescension displayed by others, the eagerness to assist and to please, that went along with being a "milady." To one who had never experienced the advantages of being a member of the gentry, her fears might seem foolish, even petty. But she was certain she was not the first milady to stand at the door of happiness, afraid to cross the threshold and enter into a new station of life.

Charlotte's thoughts turned to William Halsey, whose predicament was in some ways similar to hers. A man had the ability to raise a woman to his station in life, but only if he possessed a fortune. She wondered how steadfast a lover the young man would be after he heard about the paltry sum that had been bestowed upon Miss

Emily Steele. If the young lady was worthy of his affections, it seemed a pity, a terrible pity, that they could not marry and enjoy a life together. What crime had the two committed? Charlotte wondered, to warrant such a harsh sentence.

A smile played about her lips. She did not usually think in terms of "crimes" and "sentences." Being in the company of Mr. Bryght must have influenced her thoughts. Perhaps one day she, too, would learn how to think like a Bow Street Runner and learn how to interpret the glances and silences and see into another person's thoughts. But the next moment the smile vanished.

"Oh, no!" she exclaimed, hardly aware the words had escaped from her lips. Surely Theo Bryght could not think that!

The next morning, Theo Bryght informed Lord Lauferby that they were going to visit the Castle. In theory, the young gentleman could not object, since he was certain William Halsey would be longing for some news. But the morning had brought with it a light rain, and Lord Lauferby could not look forward to the thought of what those raindrops would do to the tops of his exquisitely polished boots. But he made the sacrifice, for the sake of friendship, and followed Bryght into the street, after their breakfast.

They were passing the entrance to a narrow side street when Bryght stopped, stared, and began to run. "Sam!" he called out to a small figure that had also started to dash down the street.

But when the Runner caught his quarry, he was disappointed to discover the frightened child was not

Sam. He gave the boy a coin, and the child scampered away.

When they reached the Castle, Theo Bryght assumed his most imposing air and announced that he had come from Bow Street, in London, to see the prisoner William Halsey. Without further ado, he and Lauferby were shown into the prisoner's small cell.

The Runner was pleased to see that prison life had not left too heavy a mark on the young man. He was paler than when Bryght had first made his acquaintance, but he still had the resilience of youth — and, perhaps, the certainty he was innocent — to help him retain his composure during his ordeal.

That composure was temporarily rattled by the Runner's first question: "Why did you kill The Miller of Dee?"

Halsey stared open-mouthed at the Runner. Then he said, "Either you have gone mad, Mr. Bryght, or you are mocking me."

"Neither, Mr. Halsey. You were seen at the Roodee on the night the horse was poisoned."

"That is impossible. I was at home that evening. My mother, Lady Halsey, will tell you that."

"She would know if you slipped out of your home at midnight and rode to Chester?"

"The groom would know."

"You mentioned only Lady Halsey. Was your father not at home that evening?"

"No, he had some business in Liverpool. He stayed there overnight."

"Yet someone did see you at the Roodee that night. He recognized your coat."

"And I tell you it is impossible."

"Do not lie to me, Mr. Halsey. If you were there for some innocent reason — or if, perhaps, you were drunk and went there to argue with your trainer or Old Peter — it is best to tell me the truth."

"I am telling you the truth. I was nowhere near the Roodee that night."

The Runner did not press further; there was more to discuss. "What was in the letter you asked Sam to deliver to Miss Steele?"

"There was no letter."

"Come, Mr. Halsey, if you intend to get yourself hanged, please tell me now so I can return to London tonight and not waste any more of my time."

Halsey scowled. But when Bryght moved in the direction of the door, he reluctantly began to talk. "I asked Miss Steele to meet me at Pemberton's Parlour, later that afternoon."

"Did you often meet there?"

"Yes. It was not unusual for ladies to promenade around the Walls — and meet their acquaintances during their walk."

"When did you discover Sam did not deliver the letter?"

"Later. At the time, it did not occur to me that Sam had not been able to deliver the letter. When I heard the news about the arrival of Miss Steele's brother — and about her father's death — I thought this was why she did not meet me. It was only after the inquest, when Sam disappeared, that it occurred to me that Miss Steele never received it."

"Where is the letter now? Did Sam return it to you?"

"No. He might still have the letter, or it might be lost."

"Do you have any idea where Sam is hiding?"

"No."

"Did you have any special way of sending for him, any secret signal?"

"There was no need. It was natural for me to visit the stable, and easy to slip him a letter."

"But that day you did not give him the letter at the stable."

For the first time, the young man looked defeated. "I do not seem to have much luck. But there was no sinister motive behind our meeting. I just happened to see him on his way to the Steele house and I gave him the letter then."

"Mr. Halsey, had did you expect to repay your creditors?"

When the young man did not reply, the Runner said, "I do not think you requested a meeting at Pemberton's Parlour, sir. I think you asked Miss Steele to elope with you to Gretna Green. Am I correct, Mr. Halsey?"

Halsey looked about to protest, but a warning glance from Lauferby changed his mind. "It was the only way! Her father would not give his permission, and with her brother due to arrive ... That was another obstacle in our path, or at least a potential one. With both her father and her brother objecting to our marriage, Emily would not have the courage to marry me. That is why I had to get her away from that house, while there was still time."

"I do not think the young woman's brother will object to your marriage, provided you are cleared of this crime."

"Have you spoken to him?"

"No, but according to the terms of the will, Miss Steele inherits only £2,500. I am sure he would like to see her happily married to a man who loves her."

William Halsey sank down onto the cot and put his head in his hands.

The Runner was sorry to see it. He would have preferred for Halsey to insist the money did not matter — that he loved the girl and wished to marry her, even without her fortune. Unfortunately, though, this was not one of those romantic novels, so popular at the time, written by "A Lady" and promising a happy ending on the final page.

Emily Steele sat in the front sitting room, stabbing unenthusiastically with her needle at a handkerchief that needed hemming. Mary and Alexander were at the shop, where they were engaged in going over the accounts with Mr. Tilson. Emily might have joined them, since she was a member of the family, too. But she had no head for figures, and she knew she would be as bored there as where she was.

She wished Julia had not returned to her room after breakfast, complaining of a headache. They might have gone for a walk. But even more than that, she wished she had received some news from William Halsey. Even though he was in prison, surely there was a way to send a message. Surely he must realize she was in agony, that she must know if her father's will had dashed their every last hope, or not.

When she heard a knock at the front door, she therefore sprang from her seat, certain the longed-for missive had arrived at last. But when the new servant entered bearing a calling card on the silver tray, she sunk back onto the settee. Listlessly, she glanced at the name. It meant nothing to her. But she saw that the card belonged to a person of rank, and so she told the servant to say she was at home.

Ella returned to the front door and, without letting on that she was well acquainted with the lady standing in the vestibule, showed Charlotte into the drawing room.

"Lady Ashe, ma'am," Ella said with great solemnity, before departing to arrange the tea tray.

"Lady Ashe, it is very kind of you to call," said Emily. "I am afraid Mr. Steele, my brother, and my sister, Miss Steele, are not at home. Mrs. Steele has taken to her bed with the headache, and I am certain she will be devastated when she learns you have called and she was not able to receive you."

Charlotte expressed the usual sentiments, as well as her condolences. This was followed by a short lull in the conversation. In that silence, Charlotte, who had decided to test her own skill at detecting, noted that Emily Steele was a pretty child, and that sadness only enhanced her ethereal beauty. She thought she could see why no one had suspected Emily Steele had poisoned her father, although Charlotte did have to admit she had only a novice's idea of what a poisoner should look like.

"I was wondering if I might be of service to you in some way," said Charlotte. "I have been detained in Chester unexpectedly, and I know so few people here. If you would care to take some exercise, I should be glad to accompany you."

"Oh, that is very kind of you, Lady Ashe," said Emily, openly expressing her liking of the suggestion. "My sister Mary has her paints to keep herself occupied, but I have only — "

She stopped in mid-sentence, but Charlotte could guess the conclusion. A young lady in love could have only one way to occupy her time.

The two arranged to meet again in the afternoon, and Charlotte left the Bridge Street home feeling very pleased with what she had accomplished. Although she had not met the entire family, she had made a good start. Indeed, she was in such high spirits she forgot to look down as she descended the short but steep staircase that led from the Bridge Street Row down to the main street and she missed a step, which sent her tumbling down to the street below. At first she was too mortified to feel pain. She therefore insisted to the curious crowd of passersby that had quickly gathered that she was quite all right. But her first step belied her too confident assertion.

"Allow me to assist you, ma'am," said a pleasant-looking young man, who offered Charlotte his arm. "Mary, can you manage with her other arm? Together we might lift her." The young man then explained, "Our home is just up these stairs."

Before she could say anything, Charlotte felt herself being lifted back up the stairs and down the Row. When Ella saw her mistress being carried between the two Steeles, she nearly gave the game away. But a look from Charlotte stopped her in time.

Emily Steele was under no such interdiction, and she exclaimed, "Lady Ashe! Whatever has happened?"

The announcement of the title had an immediate effect upon Charlotte's rescuers. Mary Steele was not one to feel inferior to anyone, but a person could not be in business without being sensitive to the benefits accrued by an association with the gentry. As for Alexander Steele, who had been raised amidst a bevy of countesses and miladies in Rome, the realization he was hosting a personage who was not part of the mercantile class quickened his interest in the unexpected visitor as well.

Charlotte allowed herself to be fussed over while a doctor was summoned. She was especially happy when Mrs. Steele put in an appearance, for now she had a complete picture of the family.

After Mr. Carlstone announced that the offending ankle was neither broken nor badly sprained, and that milady might step upon her foot gently without doing it much harm, Charlotte allowed herself to be persuaded to partake of a light nuncheon of cold meat and fruit. During the meal she managed to win the good opinion of Mary Steele even further by expressing an interest in visiting the family's shop and choosing a silk for a new dress. As for Emily and Julia, nothing further was required than a suggestion they should all take a carriage ride in the afternoon.

"Surely you prefer to rest, Lady Ashe," protested an anxious Mr. Alexander Steele. "My sister will release you from your previous engagement to take exercise this afternoon. Is that not so, Emily?"

"The fresh air will do me more good than moping in a sitting room," Charlotte assured the group, and so the excursion was settled.

Once again, Charlotte left the home, only this time more carefully. Alexander handed her into a hired carriage, which transported her back to her inn.

Mrs. Seymour, who had expected the return of her niece much earlier, did not know if she should be angry or concerned. She therefore fluctuated between both moods while she arranged a soft pillow for Charlotte's ankle and harangued her with hard reproaches, saying, "You might have sent word you were dining with the Steeles. I am nearly faint from hunger."

Instead of replying to this rebuke, Charlotte asked for her sketching pad and pencils, which Mrs. Seymour brought to the table. While the elder woman satisfied her hunger, Charlotte sketched out three portraits, which she placed upon the table.

"Do you see it, Auntie?"

Mrs. Seymour turned her attention from the plate of cold meat to the drawings. "I see three young people, Charlotte. Are we acquainted with them?"

"I met them this morning. Would you say they are related?"

Mrs. Seymour looked at the drawings more closely. "Perhaps there is a slight resemblance between the two girls about the chin. But, no, I would not necessarily guess they were from the same family. Are they?"

"They are the three Steele children."

Mrs. Seymour glanced at the drawings again, and then allowed her attention to be enticed by a piece of sponge cake. "That is often the way it is with families," she said between bites. "Either they are all exact likenesses of one another, or there is no resemblance at all. You would not know about such things, Charlotte, not having any brothers and sisters who survived past their infancy. But I can recall a family, when I was young, that had …"

While Mrs. Seymour chattered, Charlotte continued to study her three drawings. She knew it was true that siblings sometimes did not look alike, yet she was sure one of the Steele children resembled someone she knew. But the name refused to announce itself, and as for the face of that other person, it faded in and out of focus in her mind, as though it were the ghost of some mischievous Cavalier.

After they left the Castle, Theo Bryght announced to his companion that Lord Lauferby could spend the rest of the morning as he wished. The Runner intended to pay a visit to the Black Lion, an ale house where Lauferby's London dress and manners would be too conspicuously out of place.

When Bryght arrived, the ale house was not so full that the publican could not spare a few moments to speak with a customer. But either Mr. Hardwich was a naturally reticent man around strangers or his too-perceptive nose noticed something amiss about the Runner's demeanor, for he did not seem eager to linger in conversation after setting down the tankard of ale.

Bryght had decided to keep to his story that he was in Chester to view the horse Cavalier, with an eye to purchasing it for a certain gentleman. However, Hardwich would say nothing more than that it was a fine horse and Thomas Steele had looked after it very well.

"I hear Mr. Steele looked after his friends very well, too."

"You must have good ears to hear so much, considering you are a stranger to these parts."

"When a man is murdered in his home, people will talk."

The publican merely gave the counter a good wipe with his cloth. Bryght therefore tried another tack and said, "I wonder Mr. Steele did not take precautions to guard Cavalier, after that other horse was killed."

"This is an Independents public house, sir," said the owner. "If you are insinuating that Mr. Steele or any other person belonging to the Independent party had anything to do with the death of The Miller of Dee, you can take your business to the King's Arms or the Crown, where you and your opinions will feel more at home."

"The man only voiced a natural sentiment, Hardwich," said a wizened old man who had been sitting further off but now took a seat beside Theo Bryght. "But, sir, if I may be so bold to speak my mind to a stranger, you say it because you are not familiar with the Roodee. Old Peter may look like all he cares about is his pipe, but he's got sharper eyes and ears than many a man that's half his age. If he says the only person who was in the stable that night, other than Old Peter and the boy Sam, was Sir Richard Halsey, then that's what was."

It took the Runner a great deal of effort to keep his eyebrows from rising upward toward the half-timbered ceiling at this new piece of information. "Does Sir Richard also stable his horses at the Roodee? I thought it was his son who had a horse there."

"Only during the racing season. But the gentry from these parts don't stand on ceremony. They like to drop by the stable for a look round and a gossip, just like the rest of us, when they are in town."

"The stable is open to everyone, then, at all hours of the day and night? Or do you mean to say Old Peter never sleeps?"

The elderly man chuckled over some private joke. But then he said, "You're still young enough to sleep soundly in your bed. But when you get to be as old as me and Old Peter, you'll see; a mouse creeping behind the paneling is enough to wake a person up, providing he isn't stone deaf, of course."

"So Sir Richard came to the stable that evening to check up on Cavalier and share a smoke with Old Peter?"

"The Miller of Dee, you mean to say; that was the horse that belonged to Sir Richard's son."

The Runner smiled. His companion might be elderly, but he was still alert, since he caught the Runner's intentional error.

Bryght noticed that his companion's tankard was empty, and he called to the publican to fill it up. "What would you say, sir, would you purchase Cavalier, if the family was willing to sell?"

The old man shook his head. "Call me an old superstitious fool, if you like, but I don't see that neither Cavalier nor The Miller of Dee brought their owners any luck. I'd place my money on a horse without so much history and make a clean start."

After he left the Black Lion, Bryght paid a visit to Mr. Carlstone, who had only just returned from ministering to a patient. He did not bother to disguise his identity from the doctor, nor the reason that had brought him to Chester, since he wished to receive answers to questions that only a representative of the law was entitled to ask. But first, he discovered, he must play the part of audience, since the physician was on his hobby horse and was not yet ready to come down.

"The steps leading down from the Rows are treacherous, as you may have noticed," the physician commented, while he hung up his great coat and put away his medical bag. "A lady fell from the steps at Bridge Street only this morning. I have just come from there."

"She was not seriously hurt, I hope."

"She was one of the lucky ones; not even her ankle was sprained. But it is a wonder there are not more instances of people breaking their necks, especially at night, when the light is so bad."

"I shall keep that in mind," said the Runner. "Can nothing be done to remedy the situation?"

"What can we do? The only way to solve the problem of the steps is to dismantle the Rows, and what would Chester be without its Rows? Just another town, I am afraid, with nothing to distinguish it from any other town in England."

"There is the Roodee, sir," said the Runner. "And the Walls."

"True, but at the end of the day a racecourse is a racecourse, and there are other cities that have preserved at least a portion of their medieval walls. But the Rows are unique, to my knowledge, a mystery that has yet to be solved. As a Bow Street Runner, you should appreciate the significance of that."

"I had not realized the Rows presented such a puzzle."

"Well, think of it, sir. What are the Rows? A covered walkway attached to the upper floor of the buildings in the center of town. What do they accomplish? Nothing, except to block the light of day and sprain people's ankles. But do the good people of Chester insist the Rows be torn down? Not for love or money, sir. And why not?" The physician spread out his hands. "A mystery!"

"You would have the Rows torn down, I take it?"

"I would, sir. As a man of science, I prefer the light of the present day to the darkness of the past, even a romanticized version of those former days."

"What about the death of Thomas Steele? Does that belong to the light of day, or the darkness of the past?"

Mr. Carlstone stared at the Runner for a moment, and then he said, "I admit I am puzzled, sir. I cannot believe young Mr. Halsey did the deed, despite the quarrel over that horse. And as for the young Mr. Steele, it would be quite a feat for a newcomer to a house to succeed in poisoning the owner of that house within a few hours of his arrival."

"Then it was one of the daughters?"

The physician regarded the Runner with a look of haughty disdain.

"Well, someone had to have done it," said Bryght.

"Yes, that is very true. But the more I think about it, the more I am convinced it must have been an accident."

"An accident? How did you arrive at that conclusion, sir?"

"I have complained more than once about apothecaries who do not properly mark the packets they give out. My guess is that the Watson woman thought she was giving Steele a sleeping potion or something for his digestion. When the truth of her error was discovered, she tried to hide her involvement in the matter. A natural reaction for many people, I should say. That is why she threw the packet down into the cellar, and why she arranged that silly display of the alphabet tiles. Oh, I will admit at first she had me fooled. I do not mind admitting I was shocked at the state Thomas Steele was in — death by poison is an awful way to die, Mr. Bryght. His last moments must have been unbearable."

"Have you spoken to the magistrate about your theory?"

"Not yet. I should not like to publicly accuse Mrs. Watson of carelessness without proof. She is a widow, you know. How will she earn her daily bread, if it comes out she poisoned one of her patients, even though it was by mistake and really the fault of the apothecary, who should have marked that packet?"

"In the meantime, Mr. Halsey is sitting in jail."

"I will admit the Castle is not a pleasant place for a young gentleman to bide his time. But I have been assured there is not enough evidence to hang him."

The Runner gazed at the physician, wondering at the man's original mixture of cantankerous opinion and cheery optimism. It was fortunate he never tired of contemplating the mystery of the human race, since his profession gave him so many opportunities for coming into contact with yet another new and bizarre specimen.

"Mr. Carlstone, at the inquest, you mentioned there was a trace of poison in the glass."

"That is correct, sir.

"But could it have been placed in the glass later? Could the main dose of poison have been administered earlier — put in Mr. Steele's food, for example?"

"No, if it was Aconite, as I suspect, it must have been one of the last things on this earth poor Steele ingested. With a large dose, and this must have been a large dose, death is almost instantaneous. If it had been a smaller dose, Steele would have been violently ill for several hours, and I would have been summoned earlier."

"Then someone must have been in the room a few minutes before he died and handed him the glass."

"Precisely, and by her own testimony, Mrs. Watson was the last person to see Thomas Steele alive.

"When she brought him the hot water bottle."

"That is correct.

"And then she went down to the kitchen to have her supper."

"That is also correct."

"You do not see an opportunity for someone from the family to slip into Mr. Steele's room and administer the poison while Mrs. Watson was eating her mutton?"

"Must I instruct you in your trade, Mr. Bryght? Use your head, man! I already told you — when would Alexander Steele have had time to learn the ways of the house and find the right time to administer the poison? Furthermore, he knew that as the only son he must inherit. He saw with his own eyes his father had not much longer to live. Why, then, would he risk the gallows? No man in his right mind is that impatient."

Impatient. The word rung in the Runner's brain like a bell.

"And the daughters? How can you be so sure they did not do it?"

"They were devoted to their father, sir. Anyone who knew the family will tell you that. You will find no mystery on Bridge Street Row. Should you persist with your inquiries, I am confident you will reach the same conclusion that I did. It was a tragic mistake."

"One last question, sir," said Theo Bryght. "You mentioned that a young woman fell down the steps. Was it one of the Miss Steeles?"

"No, it was a visitor to Chester. A Lady Ashe."

CHAPTER XIV
TOO LATE

THEO BRYGHT KNEW HE MUST pay a visit to Mrs. Watson. Although she did not rank first in his mind as a likely suspect, the physician had succeeding in doing what he had perhaps hoped to prevent — raised the suspicions of the Runner. Someone had to have hated Thomas Steele enough to murder him. If that person had put the packet of poison in a place where the nurse was likely to reach for it, thinking it was some harmless potion, the Runner needed to know more about the daily routine of the house and who had easy access to the medicines.

But paying a sick call to Lady Ashe was an opportunity too tempting to be set aside by a visit with Mrs. Watson. He therefore armed himself with a bouquet of flowers and presented himself at her inn.

He was pleased to see that Charlotte was immobilized in her chair, with her injured foot resting upon a cushioned stool, since that allowed him to choose his own chair and bring it near, without a fear she would move away. He could not, of course, presume to examine her ankle with his hands, but his eyes could be excused for wandering to it as he expressed his concern and hopes that she was not in too much pain.

"I did not know you had so much gallantry in you, Mr. Bryght," Charlotte said, smiling, as she accepted both the flowers and his words. "I should have thought your first interest would be to know what I was doing on the Bridge Street Row."

"I had wondered, my lady."

"Today you must not 'milady' me, for I was playing a role you are familiar with. I was a Bridge Street Runner."

"A Bridge Street Stumbler, I think you mean to say, my lady. But what did you hope to discover on Bridge Street?"

"I wished to become acquainted with the Steele family."

"And so you threw yourself down the steps? That is an original way to arrange a meeting, my lady, but a bit dangerous, even for a Bow Street Runner. According to Mr. Carlstone, you might have broken your neck."

"I did not fall on purpose, but it did serve my purpose. Surely that shows I have a certain amount of cunning, which I believe is an attribute a Runner must possess to be successful."

Theo Bryght was silent.

"You do not approve?" she asked.

"Do you care if I approve, or not?"

His eyes, glints of brilliant sapphire blue, held hers, as though she was in a kind of trance. But before Charlotte could reply, Mrs. Seymour entered the room and broke the spell.

Theo Bryght was not by nature someone who cursed his fellow men over every little wrong or slight; but at that moment a few choice words directed at Mrs. Seymour did enter his mind, although he managed to barricade them behind his closed lips.

"I hope you will give my niece a good upbraiding," said Mrs. Seymour, settling herself before the fire. As she had brought her workbox with her, it was clear she did not intend to leave the room anytime soon. "I cannot think what possessed Charlotte to pay a visit to the Steeles, and to eat a meal in their home, when there is a poisoner about."

"At least let me tell Mr. Bryght what I discovered, Auntie, and then he can rebuke me as much as he wishes."

"And what did you discover, my lady?"

"This." Charlotte showed him her drawings of the Steele children. "Perhaps it is nothing, but these drawings will not let me go. Do you see what is there — or, rather, what is missing?"

He took the drawings from her hands and studied them. He did not say it, but he silently admitted her talent with a pencil — her ability to quickly sketch a face — would be useful in his profession. But he wanted a wife, not a partner. It was one thing to discuss a case with her and elicit her opinion, and quite another to envision her performing the same tasks he did, taking the same risks, descending to the same low strata of society, when the occasion demanded it.

"It is only a likeness," Charlotte was saying, "but to me it is very clear."

"It is a pity we do not have a likeness of Thomas Steele, and the mother, as well."

"Then you do see it! I thought you would."

"It may not mean anything. It is common for one sibling to favor one side of the family, while another favors the other."

"I think I might be able to obtain a sketch of Thomas Steele."

"How?"

"Mary Steele paints, or so Emily told me. Surely she painted at least one portrait of her father. I could express an interest in seeing her work, and then insist upon doing my own sketch of her father's portrait because I admire it so much."

"Charlotte!" Mrs. Seymour exclaimed. "I forbid it! I will not let you return to that house. Mr. Bryght, tell her she must not go."

He stopped for a moment to consider. A myriad of impressions — no more than half-sentences, really — swirled about his mind. He had not come to the end of the mystery; he was still far from it. But this might at least be the beginning — the piece of the puzzle that contained the clue for all that must follow.

"Your aunt is right, Lady Ashe. You must not go to that house. You must run!"

Mrs. Watson put the kettle on the fire. She then put the large hunk of seed cake she had bought in town onto a plate. The plate had a small chip, but that did not matter. It was not as if the Prince Regent was coming to tea, she chuckled to herself, or the Princess Charlotte.

She had not hurried to find another position after the death of her last employer, Thomas Steele. There would always be sickness and infirmity, should she choose to return to work. But at the moment she did not choose. She was enjoying herself, getting up late, not being at anyone's beck and call, having a second cup of tea or another slice of cake without some Cook begrudging every mouthful she swallowed.

A knock at the door interrupted her reverie. She took out the timepiece that had belonged to her dead husband and which she kept in her work pocket, and she frowned. Her visitor was early. Well, they would have to wait for their tea. A kettle could not be hurried.

Theo Bryght saw Charlotte into her hired carriage. "Do not press too hard," he advised her. "If the topic of painting does not naturally come up in the conversation today, wait until tomorrow."

"I am not a goose. I do know something about the art of conversation."

"This is different. You would like to prove you are as good at this job as I am. But I have been doing it longer than you, my lady, and I can assure you that patience ..."

He stopped. There was that word again — patience, or its adversary, impatience.

"Is something wrong?" asked Charlotte.

He shook his head. "Just promise me you will not be impatient and try to accomplish too much too quickly. Do not give yourself away."

The carriage drove off. He would have liked to call it back. A moment earlier, he had not thought Charlotte would be in any real danger at the Steele house, but now he was not so sure. His inquiries in the town had not revealed any new suspects. There were the usual squabbles between competing tradesmen, but nothing serious enough to provoke murder — and if someone out of the ordinary had visited the house on the day of Thomas Steele's death, someone would have mentioned it by now. That meant the circle of possible suspects was small: William Halsey and the Steele family and Mrs. Watson. That last person was still an unknown. He must therefore see if he could discount Mrs. Watson, along with William Halsey, to further diminish the circle.

He first returned to the Bear and Billet, to inquire about directions to Mrs. Watson's cottage. His innkeeper informed him the cottage lay outside the Walls, on the other side of the River Dee. The Watsons had always had a fiercely independent streak, said the innkeeper — and the Runner wondered if a person might find a touch of smuggling in that cottage, since in those times an independent streak was often a mask for something else, usually illegal.

But he promised himself he would not become sidetracked, while conversing with Mrs. Watson. A nurse was in an excellent position to see most of what went on inside a house, if she had good eyes in her head. And Bryght was certain the woman had very good eyes, indeed.

He was about to leave the inn when he spied Lord Lauferby fretting over a swath of linen that had been burnt by an over-zealous iron.

"The service in this inn is deplorable," the young lord lamented.

"How would you like to return to London, then?"

"You have found the murderer?"

"Not yet. But have you any acquaintances who have recently been in Italy?"

"Someone has always just returned from the Continent, Bryght. What is it you wish to know?"

"I wish to find someone who knew Alexander Steele, or his mother, in Rome."

Lord Lauferby wrinkled his nose. "A silk mercer's wife? Really, Bryght, I do not think such a person would be familiar with my acquaintances."

"Do not be so sure. Society is more free and accepting in countries like Italy, especially if Mrs. Steele was a beautiful woman with a respectable amount of wealth at her disposal."

"But what is it that you wish to know?"

"Anything that you can find out."

Bryght had only just traversed the bridge that spanned the River Dee when he was confounded by a sight that he thought must make him postpone his plans to speak with Mrs. Watson yet another time. Mary Steele, who was looking dangerously pale, was running towards him, clumsily and uncharacteristically oblivious to the sight she presented to the world.

"Mr. Bryght! Thank heavens you are here!" she exclaimed, nearly falling into his arms.

"What has happened, Miss Steele? Are you well enough to speak?"

"It is Mrs. Watson. We must call Mr. Carlstone."

"She is ill?"

Mary Steele shook her head. "She ... Oh, it is too horrible. Mrs. Watson is dead."

Theo Bryght had seen many unpleasant things during his career as a Bow Street Runner, but the contorted face that belonged to what had once been Mrs. Watson was one sight he was sure he would never forget. It was perhaps crass of him that his first thought was a regret he had postponed his interview with the woman — not because he thought he might have prevented the woman's death, but because he had lost the opportunity to question her — but that went with being a Runner. Besides, he knew all too well that when a murderer was intent on doing away with his victim, it was next to impossible to stop him. Or her.

When Mr. Carlstone had finished with his examination of the body, as well as the broken crockery scattered on the floor, the Runner said, "Well, Mr. Carlstone, are you still convinced Mr. Steele's death was an accident?"

The elderly physician shook his head. "I had not expected this."

"The symptoms are the same? There can be no question that Mrs. Watson did not die a natural death?"

"No, there is no question here. But who could have done such a thing, Mr. Bryght?"

"Perhaps the constable and his men will be able to shed some light on the matter."

Constable Merriweather arrived soon afterward. He was not an incompetent agent of the law, but it was apparent he was not happy to investigate yet another case of violent poisoning. It was not a pleasant business to gingerly examine the scene of the crime, and the officer of the law had to go outside for some fresh air on more than one occasion.

When he finished with his work, he said, "I admit it, Mr. Bryght. I am at a loss." He then added, "I know that whoever poisoned Mrs. Watson must have poisoned Mr. Steele, as well. The poor lady must have seen the murderer, and he found out about it. But I cannot believe that anyone in our town would be so ... unchivalrous."

Bryght smiled at the choice of word. Poison was not a pretty way to die. Even a woman past her prime, such as Mrs. Watson had been, would not wish to be discovered in such a disgusting state of disarray. The constable was right; this murderer lacked the chivalrous touch.

"Let us not forget our manners, as well, Constable," said Bryght. "Miss Steele is still waiting outside."

"Good heavens, you are right."

To the constable's great relief, Miss Steele did not reprimand him for keeping her waiting. On the contrary, she commended him for taking the time to make a thorough examination of the scene. "You must find this madman before he strikes again," she told him. "Leave no stone unturned."

The constable's relief faded as he looked unhappily at the stony terrain that surrounded them. To his mind, it would be an easier task to look underneath each and every one of those real stones than to examine every person in Chester and hope to discover the murderer — for that was how his task appeared to him, gigantic and, ultimately, hopeless.

"It was fortunate that you were able to alert us so quickly, Miss Steele," said the Runner.

Acknowledging the hint, she replied, "I was not in the habit of visiting Mrs. Watson, of course. But she had asked me to do her a favor and retrieve the alphabet tiles she had lent my father, for his use. Constable Merriweather allowed me to take them this morning, is that not so, Constable?"

Merriweather stammered a suitable reply.

"You did not choose to entrust the task of returning the tiles to a messenger?" Bryght asked.

"I thought a long walk would do me good."

"Do you often take long walks without an attendant, Miss Steele?"

"When I make a sketching excursion, I usually bring along one of the servants, to help with the easel and paints. But the household has been quite upside down since my father's death, and I did not wish to further upset the servants and their work."

"I am sure they appreciate your consideration, ma'am," said Merriweather, having somewhat recovered from his initial and usual discomfiture when in the presence of Miss Steele.

"Was Mrs. Watson still alive when you arrived at her home?" asked Bryght.

"No, she was not. When no one answered my knock, I would have left the boxes of tiles by her door and returned home. But I heard a kettle whistling inside, and I thought it odd that Mrs. Watson would leave her kettle on the fire, unattended. It was not like her."

"And so you went inside?"

"Yes."

"The door was not locked?"

"No."

"And you saw?"

"I saw what you and the constable saw. The only thing I did was to remove the kettle from the fire. The noise grated. In my hysteria — and I am not embarrassed to admit that I was quite overcome by what I saw."

"We understand, ma'am," said Constable Merriweather. "Anyone would have been shocked."

Miss Steele gave the officer of the law a polite nod of her head and said, "As I was saying, in those initial moments, when my faculties were disarranged, the kettle's whistle sounded to me like a woman's scream. I could not bear to hear it, and so I removed the kettle from the fire."

"You touched nothing else?"

She seemed to recoil at the very thought of it. "No, after I removed the kettle I rushed out of the house, to find help."

"Who did you see on your way to Mrs. Watson's home?"

"After I left the Walls, I do not recall seeing anyone, Mr. Bryght."

"Is that usual, for the road to be empty?"

"I did not say the road was empty. I said I do not recall seeing anyone. If some laborer or his wife happened to be on the road at the same time, there was no reason why I should take especial note of them."

"Very true, ma'am," said the constable, "although I am sure they would take great pleasure at seeing you, Miss Steele."

"And you saw no one from the time you left Mrs. Watson's home until you saw me?" asked the Runner.

"I am certain I did not, sir. I should have asked for their assistance, if I had."

Theo Bryght was silent, and in that moment Mary Steele asked if she might be allowed to return home, since the events of the day had left her fatigued.

"Permit me to drive you in my carriage, Miss Steele," said Mr. Carlstone, who had remained to supervise the removal of the body, a task which was by then completed.

"One last question, Miss Steele, before you go," said the Runner. "When you sent word to Mrs. Watson to accept her invitation to tea, why did you not send the tiles at the same time?"

"I do not understand you, sir. Mrs. Watson did not invite me to tea. She would not presume to take such a liberty."

"Yet she was expecting someone. There were two broken teacups on the ground."

"If she was expecting someone, I can assure you, Mr. Bryght, the person was not me."

CHAPTER XV
TAKEN FOR A RIDE

WHEN CHARLOTTE ARRIVED AT the Steele home, she found Emily in a state of anxiety. Her sister-in-law, who was prone to headaches, had gone to her room after lunch to rest and had awoken only a short while ago. She was now dressing and sent her apologies to Lady Ashe for the delay.

"Think nothing of me," Charlotte assured Emily. "I am only glad to hear Mrs. Steele is sufficiently recovered to join us."

While Emily anxiously wondered how she might entertain as grand a personage as Lady Ashe, Charlotte had to struggle to hide her pleasure at the opportunity presented by the delay. Attempting to sound as calm as possible, she asked, "Do you paint, by any chance, Miss Steele? There are so many interesting views of Chester that I am quite angry at myself for neglecting to bring my paint box with me. If you could direct me to a shop where I might purchase a few supplies, I should be most grateful."

Emily was quick to name a nearby shop, and then she added, "I only dabble, from time to time. It is my sister Mary who has a real talent."

"I would like to see her work someday. Does she paint landscapes or portraits?"

"Both," said Emily. "A few of her views of the Chester Rows were recently exhibited in Manchester."

Since Charlotte was not interested in that, she said, "I suppose your father must have been very proud of her. Did she ever paint his portrait?"

Charlotte felt a twinge of guilt when the young woman eagerly jumped at the bait. She could assuage her conscience only by reminding it that Miss Steele might be in great danger.

She followed Emily into the dining room. Emily apologized for the lack of sunlight, explaining it was a common problem for houses located on the Rows. After several candles were lit, there was sufficient light for Charlotte to see the portrait of Thomas Steele.

It was a large and imposing picture, which depicted the silk mercer when he was in the prime of life and in good health. There was no doubt where Mary Steele had gotten her strong features and strength of character from. But Charlotte looked in vain for a hint of a softer quality about the eyes and the mouth, something that suggested the more pliable features of the younger Miss Steele or her brother.

"It is a very good likeness," Emily offered. "But you must not think my father always looked so stern. It is an official portrait."

"Your sister never painted your father and mother together?"

Emily blushed. "My mother and my brother left England when Alexander was just a baby. It is no secret in Chester that my parents did not have a happy marriage. I believe my father destroyed any pictures he might have had of my mother."

"I lost both of my parents when I was young," said Charlotte. "Having their portraits was a great comfort to me. I am sorry you did not have anything to remind you of your mother."

"I am sometimes told I resemble her," said Emily. She then added, "I wish my brother had brought her picture with him. I should have liked to see it. But I suppose young men are not sentimental in the way we are."

When they returned to the drawing room, Julia Steele was waiting for them. The visitor from Italy had wrapped herself in a voluminous cloak with a ruffed hood that fit snugly around her head, leaving only the minutest glimpse of her visage.

"I am not yet used to your English climate," she explained.

Emily had thought to suggest a drive by the River Dee, but a worry that the air might be too damp for Julia made her hesitate.

"Dearest Emily, between the river and the canal it is impossible to escape the damp air, I think," said Julia. "But I am prepared to do battle with your English weather, am I not?"

Both Charlotte and Emily agreed the Italian cloak would do admirably, and they set out. Julia Steele seemed to be truly glad of Charlotte's company, and she readily answered the polite questions put to her about her life in Italy. But even though it was interesting to both of the English ladies to hear about the skill of the dressmakers and the elegance of the homes and the wonderful concerts Julia had known and enjoyed in Rome, she could not offer much information about the former Mrs. Steele — the mother of Emily and Mary and Alexander.

"I went to school in Switzerland," she explained. "I met my husband not long after Mrs. Steele passed away. Perhaps he should have waited until the year of mourning was completed, but he was alone. He had no family in Rome. And I think it is hard for a young man to be on his own, especially a man like Alexander."

Charlotte wondered what sort of support and comfort a pretty bauble like Julia Steele could give her husband. But perhaps the young man had enough inner resources of his own, and so all he needed was a wife who made a fuss over him and looked elegantly alluring.

That was the picture Charlotte was drawing in her mind of the former Mrs. Steele, the wife of Thomas Steele — a young woman who possessed Emily's gentle beauty and enjoyed company and gaiety — and had married a man who cared only for his business and his social position in provincial Chester. Yet while many women who married unwisely lived with their decision and found their happiness in their children, Mrs. Steele had run off to Italy with her youngest child. That act suggested that either she was a woman of spirit or a madwoman, and Charlotte wondered if she would ever be able to discover the truth.

A slight cry from Emily made both Charlotte and Julia Steele turn.

"What is it?" asked Charlotte.

"Please, stop the carriage!" exclaimed Emily, who had already made a movement to open the door. A moment later she jumped down to the pavement and began to run. "Sam!" she cried out. "Stop, please! Sam!"

Charlotte caught sight of a child who was running away with all his might. But Emily's outcry had caused several of the passersby to join in the chase. One of them, a young soldier, grabbed Sam by the collar and hauled him back to Emily.

"Here he is, ma'am. Has he stolen anything from you? Shall I bring the young ruffian to the constable?"

Emily looked flustered. Charlotte, who had alighted from the carriage and joined Emily, replied in her stead, "Thank you, but there is no need. He has run away. We will return him to his home." She then placed her own gloved hand on Sam's collar and said, "Come along. Cook has been worried sick."

Sam was none too happy about being shoved into the carriage — his suggestion that he should ride with the coachman was vetoed by Charlotte, who feared he might try again to make his escape — and once inside he sat as close to the edge of the machine as he could manage.

Charlotte could see that despite the child's bravely sullen front he was scared to death, and so she tried to allay his fears, saying, "You are among friends, Sam. We will not allow anyone to harm you."

He did not look convinced. Instead, he turned to Emily and said, "Don't let them take me to the Castle, Miss Emily. I meant no harm."

"Sam, what happened to the letter? Have you got it?" asked Emily.

"The letter, Miss?"

"Yes. The letter Mr. Halsey gave you the day my father died. Where is it?"

"It's gone, Miss."

"Gone? What do you mean, Sam? How can it be gone?"

"I always hid the letters inside the lining of my cap, Miss. And I've lost my cap." The boy raised his hand to his head, which was indeed bare of any covering.

"You cannot have lost it," Emily insisted, growing increasingly hysterical. "You cannot! It cannot be lost! It cannot!"

"Emily, dear, do not upset yourself so," said Julia, putting her arm around the sobbing girl.

Perhaps it was a trick of the light, but Charlotte thought she saw a momentary smile pass across the face of the new Mrs. Steele.

Alexander Steele was sitting in the former study of Thomas Steele when he heard his wife lead a still sobbing Emily up the stairs. He did not go out into the hallway; he was certain Julia could take care of this latest outburst and he preferred to continue with his perusal of a large and heavy account book.

When Julia entered the room a half hour later, she said, "They found the stable boy. But the letter is lost."

"Hence the tears from Emily?"

"I did not know English girls could be so emotional."

"You are sure the letter is lost?"

"The boy from the stable insists it is so. It was in his cap, and the cap is gone."

"So is Mrs. Watson."

"The nurse? She has disappeared?"

"She is dead."

Julia gave a start. "How?"

"Poisoned. Mary discovered the body, apparently. She came home quite upset — for Mary, that is."

"I do not understand."

"It seems Mary went to Mrs. Watson's cottage earlier today, to return those alphabet tiles. But the woman was already dead when Mary arrived."

"She was a foolish woman, that nurse."

"And the magistrate will be a foolish man if he continues to hold Mr. Halsey in prison — unless it is the custom in Chester to allow prisoners to leave the premises of their jail to commit a murder or two."

Julia went to the table where Alexander was sitting and glanced back down at the page he had been studying. "How long will it take to sell the contents of this house?"

"You are impatient to return to Italy?"

"You know I am. This is not a happy house."

Alexander laughed.

Tea was brought into the study, since it was for only Julia and Alexander; the two sisters were still upstairs, presumably resting in their rooms. Julia sniffed suspiciously at the plate of cakes, to the amusement of her husband.

"Poison does not usually have a smell, Julia. How many times have I told you that?" He took a cake and bit into it with relish. "The cook is quite a good baker, for an Englishwoman."

"I do not see how you can be so unconcerned."

"That is because you refuse to listen, my dear. It is most unlikely he murderer of Mr. Steele will use the same means to do away with you and me. I am more concerned about getting a nasty bump on the head or, should the culprit be more original, a deadly spider in the post. But I will not give this person the satisfaction of seeing me starve myself to death out of fear the sugar sprinkled on the cook's excellent cakes is actually poison."

To prove his point, he took another cake and hungrily devoured it. Julia, however, eschewed the tea tray and drifted toward the fireplace, the one bright spot in the otherwise dark and sunless room, which was made even darker by its dark and heavy furniture that dated back to an earlier time. Those outdated furnishings included a silent companion, this one of a youthful Cavalier. The trompe l'oeil amused Julia, just as it had amused seventeenth-century ladies and gentlemen before her.

"His eyes seem to follow one, do they not?" Julia walked across the room, casting a glance behind her after every few steps.

"How can he help but admire you, my darling?" said Alexander, raising his eyes from his teacup. "You are the prettiest thing to enter this house in years."

"Lady Ashe is an elegant woman."

Alexander frowned. "What is your opinion of her, Julia? I cannot believe she is truly interested in cultivating a friendship with a silly goose like Emily, but I cannot think of another reason for her visits."

"Perhaps she is bored."

"Why then does she not leave Chester? What is she doing here?"

"She did not say," said Julia.

"Try to find out the next time you see her."

Their conversation was interrupted by the ringing of the front door's bell. Alexander went into the hallway, where he saw Mr. Tilson standing in the foyer, speaking with the new parlor maid.

Ella was about to go upstairs, when Alexander came forward to greet Mr. Tilson. "You wished to see me, sir?" he asked.

Mr. Tilson glanced up to the top of the staircase. "I wished to speak with Miss Steele, sir, about a new order of silk."

"You may ask me. Miss Steele is resting."

"It is not strictly a business matter, sir. It is about a new pattern. I wished to have a lady's opinion about it, before I place an order."

"Have you brought a sample? My wife can take a look at it."

Mr. Tilson hesitated. "Yes, Mr. Steele, she could. But she is not from Chester, sir, and so she would not know what the ladies here like."

"Then you must send round a message another time. Miss Steele cannot be disturbed."

Mr. Tilson bowed and left. Alexander was about to return to the study, when he saw Mary Steele standing at the top of the staircase.

"I am perfectly able to decide who I wish to see, Mr. Steele," she said.

The young man laughed. "Oh, Mary, do not be so frosty with me. I truly thought you were resting. But you must get used to the idea that I am now the master of this house, and it is I who decides who will enter it and who will not. Mr. Tilson is an employee of the family business, not our social equal. He should have sent a message."

"Mr. Tilson was always welcome in this house, during our father's time. If he is no longer welcome, then I ..."

Alexander gave her a quizzical look. "Then what, Mary?"

When she did not reply, he said, "I fear you are still distressed by this morning's events. I shall have some beef broth sent to your room."

He turned and began to walk down the hall, toward the study. But his alert eyes caught a glimpse, through the half-opened door, of a figure in the drawing room.

"Why are you in this room, Ella?"

"I thought you and Mrs. Steele might like a fire, sir."

"Why would we want that, if we are taking tea in the study?" He then added, "You are not employed in this household to think, Ella. Please remember that."

Ella gave a quick bob, and said, "Yes, sir."

"And, Ella, please remember that you are not employed here to listen through half-opened doors, either."

When Mary returned to her room, she could barely contain her rage. She was tempted to throw her silver-backed hairbrush at the window or the mirror, just to hear the sound of the crash. But she would not give her brother that satisfaction. By the time Ella brought up the tray with the beef broth, Mary was seated in her usual chair, with a book in her hand.

Emily had seen the servant bring the tray, and after Ella departed she knocked on Mary's door and entered the room.

"Are you not well?" Emily asked.

"I am perfectly well," Mary replied. "I believe I am being punished — or worse."

"If you would only give Alexander a chance."

"A chance to do what? It seems to me he has settled quite nicely into his new role."

Mary lifted the cup with the broth and crinkled her nose. She then dipped her little finger into the liquid and gingerly brought her fingertip to her lips.

"Mary, what are you doing? You cannot think the broth is poisoned!"

"You, too, intend to tell me what I may and may not think and do?"

Emily blushed. "Of course not. But why should anyone wish to poison you?"

Mary pushed the cup in Emily's direction. "You drink it, Emily. I have no appetite."

When Emily did not take the cup, Mary smiled. "That is how things stand, is it? You cannot believe your new-found brother would harm our father or you, but you do believe I might have slipped some poison into this cup before you came in."

"How can you say such a thing?"

"Would you like to search my room, Emily? Perhaps you will discover where I hide the packets. I am sure Alexander and that doll-wife of his would enjoy seeing me hang, although the sight might be too indelicate for your weak eyes."

Emily seized the cup from Mary's hand and drank down the broth in three gulps. "I would rather die than let myself go mad from hate," said Emily, replacing the cup on the tray. "I would rather die!"

CHAPTER XVI
TOWER AND CASTLE

IN OTHER CIRCUMSTANCES, Sam would have been happy to see Theo Bryght, for the memory of the hearty breakfast in the inn was a dear one to the child. But even though the Runner had ordered a meal of mutton and peas and sat the boy down in the chair closest to the fire, it was all too apparent that Sam had other things on his mind, namely lifelong imprisonment in the Castle.

"Sam, I shall pack you in my trunk and carry you away to London, before I let anyone in Chester harm you," said Theo Bryght.

"What should I do in London?" asked the boy, his eyes opening wide. "And how can I leave Old Peter? Who will sweep the stable when his aches and pains get bad and he cannot hold the broom?"

"Then you must help me help you, by telling me what you know."

"Perhaps the child is tired," said Lady Ashe, who had brought Sam to the Bear and Billet — and relished the surprised look on Theo Bryght's face when she escorted the boy into the inn.

"I am sure he is," Bryght replied. "But I cannot risk losing him a second time." He then said to Sam, "Try to think. Where were you when you noticed you had lost your cap?"

Sam expressed his reluctant cooperation by shoveling a fork filled with mutton and peas into his mouth, chewing the food slowly while he made a show of thinking deeply about the matter. Finally, he said, "I was in the vault, sir, under the Bridge Street Row. I remember feeling the letter pressing down on the top of my head and wondering how a little thing like that could cause so much trouble."

"Why did you not tell Mr. Halsey you had his letter that morning when we met you on the Walls? Why did you not return it to him then?"

Sam took another bite of mutton and peas while he considered the question. "If I recall correctly, sir, it was because I was mightily afraid. Fear does funny things to a person."

"You do not strike me as the sort who takes fright easily, Sam. You must have a pretty cool head to have risked raising the ire of Mr. Thomas Steele, should your role of playing postman have been found out."

"Delivering letters to Miss Emily was different, sir. The way I see things is like this: a stable boy like me most likely wouldn't be hanged for delivering love letters between a gentleman and his lady. The lady's father might give me a whipping, but I didn't have to worry about that happening with Mr. Steele, since he could barely raise his hand to push away a fly. But when I heard Mr. Steele had been poisoned and people coming to the stable were saying they had heard I was in the room and hinting that maybe I had something to do with it, the letter flew out of my head, in a manner of speaking, and I didn't recall it until the night after the inquest, when I was hiding in a vault under the Rows and I took off my cap and I felt a bulky bulge under the lining."

The Runner let the boy eat some more of his food before he asked his next question: "Was it you, Sam, who knocked over the barrel in the vault underneath the Steele's home a few days ago?"

"I wouldn't have done it, sir, if it hadn't been so dark and that foolish girl hadn't yelped," Sam replied. He then looked over at Lady Ashe. "Beg pardon, ma'am. No offense intended, but some women do scream at every little thing, as though a mouse ever did a person any harm."

"I am sure Lady Ashe has not taken offense," said the Runner, glancing in her direction. "My lady is not the sort to scream. Go on with your story."

"So when I heard footsteps scurrying overhead, I decided it was time for me to get away. I'd have to try to hide the letter another day."

"In the vault?"

"Yes, sir. I thought to hide it there and then tell Miss Emily where she could find it."

"What happened next?"

"I was nearly caught by some servant girl."

Charlotte and Theo Bryght exchanged glances. If only Ella had caught Sam, the letter would have already been retrieved.

"But I ran to the window and lifted myself up, before she could get her hands on me," Sam continued. "Then I ran down the alleyway and kept running until I was all the way to King Charles's Tower. I hid there for a while, until it got dark, and then I got cold and so I went down to the bank, by the canal, and got myself under some leaves and that's where I spent the night. And in the morning, I was off again, but I suppose my cap got separated from my head during the night, without my noticing it. And I was very sorry to lose it, because I have not got another."

"We shall get you a new cap, Sam," said Lady Ashe. "But we must find that letter. If we can find it, it will clear both you and Mr. Halsey."

"You mean people won't think I killed Mr. Steele, ma'am?"

"Yes, that is exactly what I mean."

Sam regarded her with some interest, as though trying to decide if her word could be trusted or not. "Are you a Bow Street Runner, too, ma'am? I never heard of a lady Runner."

"Let us say I am learning the profession," replied Lady Ashe. "But I am correct, am I not, Mr. Bryght? If we find the letter and its contents agree with Mr. Halsey's account, surely the magistrate will let Mr. Halsey go free — and clear Sam of all suspicion."

"I should think so," replied Bryght. "As you yourself said, Sam, a man was never hanged for delivering a love letter."

Sam finished the last of the mutton while he considered the truth of his own statement. Finding no fault in the argument, he told his hosts he was now willing to show them where the cap was hidden.

"You knew where it was all the time?" Charlotte exclaimed.

"He was wise to see first if we were friends or foes," said the Runner, fearful that Sam might change his mind at any sign of renewed trouble. "Mr. Halsey was right to trust him."

Without further ado, Sam informed them that they must proceed to the Phoenix Tower, and so that is where they turned their steps. "King Charles stood at the top of that Tower during a famous battle," the boy proudly told his companions, as he led the way. "He saw his army get cut to bits, it was that big of a defeat. But the King was here in Chester, and that's no lie. When you walk up the steps to the top of the Tower, you're walking in the footsteps of royalty."

It was hard to imagine that royalty or anyone else had paid the Tower a visit in a very long while, since the small structure was in a state of sorry disrepair. Theo Bryght suggested Charlotte remain outside — there was no point in her dirtying her walking costume or risking another tumble down an uneven flight of steps. She reluctantly agreed, realizing it was more important to find the letter than to argue about her ability to climb a spiral staircase.

Sam continued to lead the way, while the Runner followed. When they came to a small landing, Sam pointed out a few abandoned trunks that smelled of rotting wood. The boy lifted the top of one of them, and the air became even fouler. After a few minutes of rummaging through the trunk's deteriorating contents, he removed a cap from the pile. He was about to hand it to the Runner when a woman's cry stopped them both.

"Charlotte!" Theo Bryght ran down the steps, and Sam followed close behind him.

When they were outside the Tower, Charlotte was nowhere to be seen. A rustling sound made them glance down toward the bank of the canal, which was covered with fallen leaves. A moment later, Charlotte's head popped out of a pile of those leaves, as she raised herself to a sitting position.

"Next time," she said, gazing up at the promenade, where Theo Bryght and Sam were standing and looking down at where she had fallen, "you may wait outside, Mr. Bryght."

While the Runner clambered over the wall and jumped down to the bank, Charlotte debated whether or not she should play the role of the fragile "My Lady," or admit she was more shaken by her adventure than hurt. It would be nice to have an excuse to lean on the Runner's shoulder, she thought, as they walked slowly back to her inn. But when she saw Sam's anxious eyes, she decided that setting the child's troubled mind at ease must come before her own pleasures. She therefore only allowed the Runner to help her up, and then she retrieved her hand from his grasp.

"Fortunately, for my bones, if not my pelisse, these leaves make a soft cushion," she said. "Did you find the letter?"

"First tell me what happened."

"I am not quite sure I know. I was looking over the wall, to the canal down below, and admiring the view, when I felt a blow to the back of my head. I think I must have lost consciousness for a moment, because the next thing I knew, I was down here, by the canal."

"You did not see who struck you?"

"No. He must have followed us, without our knowing."

Theo Bryght nodded. It was true. He had been so anxious to retrieve the letter that he had neglected to obey the first rule of a Bow Street Runner: keep your eyes open, all the time and in every direction.

"Are you sure you are not hurt?" he anxiously inquired. "If you are feeling dizzy or your vision is at all blurred, I must take you to Mr. Carlstone at once."

"I think I was more stunned than hurt by the blow. But did you find the letter?" asked Charlotte.

Bryght looked up to where the boy was still standing. "Sam, do you care to join us?"

The boy leaped down into the leaves with pleasure. He then proceeded to remove the letter from the lining of his cap and handed it to the Runner.

"You gave us a fright, ma'am," he said, while the Runner quickly read the letter's contents. "But that's all right. Anyone who fell off these walls would give a shout."

"Thank you, Sam," said Charlotte, with suitable dignity. "I am glad I have not lowered my sex in your eyes."

The Runner was satisfied that the letter agreed with William Halsey's account, but there was still one more matter that needed to be clarified. "Sam, did anyone else give you anything to deliver to the Steele house? Perhaps a packet from an apothecary that contained a sleeping potion or a digestive aid?"

"You needn't beat around the bush, sir. It's the poison you want to know about, isn't it?"

"Yes, it is. If someone knew you paid regular visits to the house, they might give you something to take there. You might not have thought anything about it, at the time."

Sam shook his head. "I should have remembered, sir. I am a stable hand, not a messenger boy, and I only delivered letters for Mr. Halsey because he had a horse stabled at the Roodee. It was a sort of favor I did for the gentleman, seeing how I was going to the Steele house anyway, to visit Mr. Steele." He then added, magnanimously, "I would have done the same for Mr. Steele, if he needed any letters delivered."

"So you did not drop an apothecary's packet? Or see one on the floor of the vault under the Steele home?"

Sam again shook his head in the negative.

"And what about the packet Sir Richard Halsey dropped in the stable, on the night The Miller of Dee died? Did you take it to Stanley House, or did Sir Richard send a messenger for it?"

"I don't recall him dropping anything in the stable, sir."

"Ah," said the Runner. "Perhaps I made a mistake, and he dropped it somewhere else."

When they reached the home of the magistrate, that gentleman was at his dinner and none too happy to be disturbed. But the combination of Bow Street and Stanley Hall — not to mention the presence of Lady Ashe — made him rise from the table and accompany the group to his study, where he removed his spectacles from his coat pocket and took the letter from Theo Bryght's hand.

"There is no date on this, Mr. Bryght," said the magistrate, after reading the letter's contents. "How can we be sure this is, indeed, the thing Mr. Talbot saw being handed to this boy?"

"A cap is not a postman's bag," replied the Runner. "It can contain only so much, and I saw Sam remove this letter from his cap's lining with my own eyes. And there is the matter of Mrs. Watson's death. Mr. Halsey could not have committed that crime."

"He could if he were working with an accomplice, sir," said the magistrate, shooting a stern glance in Sam's direction. "I must confer with my colleagues and receive their opinion."

"We shall wait," said Charlotte.

"But, my lady, the inconvenience," the magistrate protested. "Surely you will be more comfortable at your inn."

"And I am sure Mr. Halsey would be more comfortable in his home. But while he remains the Castle's prisoner, I shall remain yours."

The Runner forced himself to hide a smile, while the magistrate stammered and stared. Finally, the man waddled to his desk to compose a message to his colleagues, requesting an urgent meeting.

The Chester worthies duly arrived, complaining and protesting all the way from the front door to the magistrate's study. While they discussed this new evidence, Charlotte and Theo Bryght and Sam waited in a small sitting room, which had the advantage of a good-sized fire blazing in the hearth. Although Sam was determined to keep his wits about him, should he need to flee at a moment's notice, he was no match for the warming comfort of the room. He sank down onto the carpet, before the hearth, and almost immediately fell into an exhausted sleep.

Charlotte put a cushion under the child's head. Then she said to the Runner, "Why did you ask the child about Sir Richard? Do you suspect him of poisoning Thomas Steele?"

"There seems to be a difference of opinion about which Halsey was seen at the stable the night The Miller of Dee died, the father or the son."

"Does it matter?"

"According to William Halsey, his father was in Liverpool the night."

"Oh."

They were silent while Charlotte thought over this new piece of information. "Sam might have thought you meant William Halsey. He was exhausted."

Theo Bryght looked down at the sleeping child. "Sam has a good head on his shoulders. I think he heard me correctly, although he was probably too tired to be on his guard."

Charlotte adjusted the fire screen, so the fire would not burn too hotly on the child's face. "Must you always trick people into saying things they do not mean to say, trapping them when they are most vulnerable?"

The Runner took her hand and raised it to his lips. "Sometimes it is the only way."

By the end of the evening, Sam was informed that he could return to the Roodee, and a message was sent to the Castle to release William Halsey from his prison cell. Theo Bryght insisted that neither of those two places were suitable for a lady to visit, and so Charlotte reluctantly agreed to return to her inn.

The Runner escorted Sam back to the stable, where Old Peter tearfully welcomed the boy as if he were the old man's son. The emotional reunion came to an end when Old Peter remembered his rheumatism and began to berate the child for leaving him in the lurch for so long; there was a whole row of stalls that needed to be thoroughly swept out and no one to do the work. Sam cheerfully took up a broom, while Old Peter happily barked out his orders, and that is how the Runner left them.

The Castle was only a few minutes' walk away, and the Runner arrived at the gates of that sorry place just as William Halsey was leaving the courtyard.

"Is this your doing, Mr. Bryght? If so, I thank you."

"It is Sam you must thank, sir. He was a faithful messenger, and your letter has been found and deposited with the magistrate. But I suggest you do not use the boy to deliver your letters again."

There was an awkward silence. Then the Runner bowed slightly and took his leave. But he did not race away, since he was curious to see what the young man would do during these first few moments of freedom. To Bryght's disappointment, Halsey did not turn in the direction of Bridge Street and the Steele home. Instead, the young man hailed a passing carriage and told the driver, "Stanley Hall."

CHAPTER XVII
A SKETCHY IMPRESSION

MR. TILSON STOOD BEHIND THE counter of the silk mercer's shop. It was the end of the day, and the last customer had gone. It was his custom to inspect the premises, before locking up, to make sure everything had been properly put away and all was ready for the next day's business.

"That bolt does not belong with the spotted muslins," he said to one clerk, while to another he commented, "These scissors are dull. How do you expect to cut an even line?"

The clerks hurried to set things right. No one questioned his authority. He had been acting as manager of the business ever since Thomas Steele first became ill. And everyone knew he had the backing and approval of Miss Mary Steele, who had been her father's confidant and assistant.

There were those who whispered that the relationship between Miss Steele and Mr. Tilson, who was a bachelor, was not entirely confined to the silk business. But to their frustration, the pair had never been caught in the office or warehouse entwined in a passionate embrace. Therefore, the rumors remained just that — rumors.

When Mr. Tilson was satisfied that all was in order, he dismissed the staff. He then extinguished the remaining lights and left, locking the door behind him. It was a chilly evening, grey and damp. Usually, he would have hurried up Bridge Street and continued up Northgate Street without stopping, until he reached his rooms, which were located on King Street, near the northernmost stretch of the Walls. But this evening he stopped before the Bridge Street Row and gazed up in the vicinity of Number 10.

Sometimes, Mary Steele would be sitting on the balcony, with her easel and paints. She often painted the Rows; indeed, she had made something of a name for herself as a Chester artist. This evening, however, she was not there.

"Mr. Tilson, good evening," said Mr. Carlstone. "How is that cough of yours? Better I hope."

"Much better," replied Mr. Tilson.

"Good, but do not linger in this air," said the physician. "This is a night for a warm fire and a hot rum toddy. Good night, sir."

"Good night."

Mr. Tilson gave one last glance at the empty Row, and then he took the doctor's advice and went home.

Charlotte knew she had been neglecting her aunt, and she was determined to make amends that evening. But Mrs. Seymour was not in the mood for cards or reading aloud.

"Something is not right," said Mrs. Seymour. "I can feel it in my bones. I do wish Ella had returned. I do not like it that she is in that house."

Charlotte glanced at the clock. It was still too early for Ella to leave Bridge Street, not that there was any set time when Ella did finish her duties at the Steele home for the night. As the mistress of her own house, Charlotte knew that a house did not always run according to schedule. If the Steeles were having guests for dinner, Ella would have to stay to help serve the meal and clean up afterward.

She explained all this to Mrs. Seymour, who calmed down enough to do some sewing. This allowed Charlotte to work on her sketch of Thomas Steele. And so the evening passed, albeit more slowly than they would have liked.

When Theo Bryght reached the Steele home — for he had decided someone must personally inform Emily Steele that William Halsey had been released from prison, before she heard it being gossiped about in the shops — he was surprised to see it was not Ella who opened the door. Of course, he could not question the servant who did let him inside, since Margaret and the other servants were not supposed to know Ella was working for a Bow Street Runner.

He was shown into the drawing room, but he was in for another disappointment since it was not Emily Steele who joined him a few minutes later.

"Our home has been topsy-turvy today," said Alexander Steele. "My sisters have retired early for the night."

"I wished to inform the family that Mr. Halsey has been released from prison," said Bryght.

"I am sure at least one member of the family will be very happy to hear it."

"I should think every Englishman would be happy to see an innocent man go free."

"I agree with you in theory, sir. But our family is in a peculiar position. If Mr. Halsey did not poison my father, it means someone else did. I can only hope and pray that this madman — or madwoman — does not strike again." He then added, "My wife is quite distressed by all this, and to make matters worse the English climate does not agree with her. It is most inconvenient that we must remain in Chester until the murderer is found. I would therefore have been much happier if that was the news you had brought us — that you had found the murderer."

"I apologize for the delay, and the English climate," said the Runner, not bothering to hide his sarcasm.

As he regarded the heir of the murdered man, Bryght felt a twinge of revulsion pass over him. It was the same feeling as the one he had experienced when he saw William Halsey ride away in his hired coach. Perhaps he was getting old, for he felt he could not understand these young men, who seemed so cold and calculating even in personal matters, when they should be warmly and sympathetically concerned.

"Do you and Mrs. Steele intend to return to Italy?"

"That is our home."

"It is none of my business, but what will happen to the silk mercer business?"

"You are correct. It is none of your business. But since I will soon begin making arrangements to sell it, it will no longer be a secret and so you may as well know. Although I presume you have no interest in buying it."

"No." Theo Bryght glanced over at a picture that was hanging over the hearth, which showed a jockey and horse in motion, racing around the Roodee. "If I should buy anything in Chester, it would be Cavalier. Do they enjoy horse racing in Italy?"

Steele gave the Runner a look of disdain. "I would not know. My interests lie in other spheres."

"You will not then take the horse with you?"

"I have already sent a message to the stable that I wish to sell Cavalier. But perhaps I will take that picture with me for a souvenir, to remind me of dear old Chester, the sad and dreary home of my ancestors."

While the cook put away the last of the food from the servants' supper, Margaret and Rose dried the dishes.

"I cannot think what has come over me," said Ella, who was sitting by the fire. Her limbs felt extremely heavy and she could barely keep open her eyes.

"You will sleep here tonight, Ella," said the cook. "Margaret will not mind sharing her bed for one night."

"Of course not," Margaret agreed.

"I shall be better in a few minutes," Ella protested.

But the minutes passed and when it was time for the servants to retire for the night, Ella was already fast asleep. The cook and Margaret lifted her between them and carried her up the stairs, with Rose lighting the way with a candle, until they reached the upper level, where the servants slept. Rose retired to her room, which was more like a closet than a bed chamber, and after the two women were sure Ella was comfortable, they also went to bed. Soon they were all fast asleep.

Ella was never sure what it was that awoke her. Indeed, she had been in such a deep, dreamless sleep that when she did awake she had no idea if it was night or day, or where she was. It took her several minutes until she understood that she was in Margaret's bed chamber and a few more until she recalled she had felt unwell earlier in the evening. By the time she understood all that she was fully awake and her one thought was how to leave the Steele home undetected, so she could return to the inn of her mistress, who was surely worried by her absence.

A thin sliver of moon was casting a pale glow upon the world, and there was just enough light streaming through the small window for Ella to retrieve her clothing and get dressed, without stumbling over any furniture in the unfamiliar room. Her intention was to creep down to the kitchen and unbolt the back door — and pray that the next morning the cook would not berate her for leaving the Steele house in an unlocked state for half the night.

She had successfully navigated the first set of stairs, the ones that led from the servants' floor to the floor that housed the sleeping quarters of the family, when she heard a noise that made her stop and hold her breath. It was a strange sound for that time of night; it almost sounded like someone was dragging some heavy object through the house. She supposed there was some logical, rational reason for the noise. But she had sat in the kitchen for too many hours, listening to the cook's stories about Chester ghosts — particularly the ghosts of fallen Cavaliers, who apparently ambled through Chester homes with amazing freedom, searching for lost heads or lost lovers, or both — to not feel weak with fear.

Whatever it was — whether human, animal, or a creature from another realm—it was coming up the front staircase, slowly and stealthily. The dragging noise had stopped, but it was replaced by the sound of an almost imperceptible thud, thud, thud as the being mounted each step.

Ella, who was standing at the top of the back stairs used by the servants, tried to press her trembling body as flat as she could against the wall, feverishly alternating between a strong desire to see what it was that was causing her terror and an equally fervent wish to close her eyes and wait until the danger had passed. In the end, her courage won out and she stretched her head out from her hiding place so she could see the source of her terror when it reached the top of the stairs.

The same sliver of moon that had dimly illuminated Margaret's bed chamber had discovered the small skylight that topped the Steele home, and a pale grey beam of light wanly illuminated the top of the staircase. When the intruder's face came into the ghostly light, Ella's courage failed her. She darted back into her hiding place, scarcely daring to breathe, hoping the sound of her wildly beating heart would not alert the intruder of her presence. A moment later there was the sound of a scuffle, followed by a woman's scream.

The house awakened in an instant. Doors opened, flickering candles cast their eerie shadows on the walls, and Ella raced down the corridor to join the others, who were staring down in horror at the bottom of the stairs, where two figures lay in a tangled heap. One was Mary Steele. The other was the mutilated body of a Cavalier.

CHAPTER XVIII
THE SILENT COMPANION SPEAKS

MR. CARLSTONE WAS NOT GOING to take any chances, and he said as much to the members of the Steele family, who were all very wide awake and all gathered in the drawing room, despite the late hour. "If you will not allow me to call for the constable, I will no longer be able to render my services as a physician," he told the assembled group. He then glanced at the pale figure reclining on the sofa, "I am sorry, Miss Steele. I know how you abhor gossip about the family. But there have been too many strange occurrences in this house lately."

"He is right, Mary," said the young woman's brother. "If you prefer that we send for that Bow Street Runner from London, we will do so. But someone must be called in."

Mary Steele groaned slightly as she tried to move into a more comfortable position. "Very well," she whispered, before turning her face to the pillow.

When Theo Bryght was escorted into the room, Constable Merriweather and his men were already there. Mr. Carlstone explained to the representatives of the law that he had been summoned to the house to attend to Miss Steele, who had fallen down the stairs.

"Where exactly did you find Miss Steele?" asked the Runner.

"At the bottom of the stairs, on the floor," replied Mr. Carlstone.

"We did not think it wise to move her, until the doctor examined her," explained Alexander Steele. "We were afraid she might have been injured."

"And did Miss Steele suffer any injuries?" asked Bryght.

"I fear she may have fractured a rib or two," said Mr. Carlstone. "It is a miracle she is not more severely injured than she is. With a fall like that she might have broken her neck."

Theo Bryght nodded and then he went over to the sofa. "Are you sure you are strong enough tonight, ma'am, to answer a few questions?"

"Mr. Carlstone has informed me the pain will be even greater tomorrow," said Mary Steele.

"Very well, then, can you tell us what happened?"

Mary took a breath and grimaced from the pain. When she spoke, her voice was uncharacteristically raspy, as though she was struggling to catch her breath. "I heard a noise. I put on my dressing gown and went out into the corridor. I waited a moment, to listen. When I heard nothing, I approached the staircase. That is when I saw it."

"Saw what?" asked the Runner.

When Mary did not reply, her brother said, "Do not be embarrassed. Anyone would have been startled."

"I am not embarrassed," Mary said defiantly. "Whoever put that silent companion at the top of the stairs meant to startle someone — and send her hurtling to her death."

"You frighten me," said Julia Steele, who was visibly shivering under her light dressing gown. She then turned her large brown eyes on Theo Bryght and said, "Mr. Bryght, you must find this fiend before he kills us all. If you do not do it soon, I fear we shall all go mad. I know at least I shall."

Alexander walked over to his wife and put his arm around her. While Mary looked at the pair with evident disgust, Emily Steele, who was sitting off to the side, kept her eyes on the carpet. It was anything but the picture of a happy family scene.

"We should take a look at this silent companion before we proceed," the Runner said to the constable.

"It has not been moved," said Mr. Carlstone. "I instructed the servants to touch nothing. The hall and the staircase are now more brightly lit, but that is the only change."

While the Runner and Constable Merriweather inspected the painted figure of the Cavalier, the constable said, "It don't look like much in this light, but I can see how it might give a person a fright when it's dark and a person isn't expecting to meet another body on the stairs."

Bryght agreed. The figure was startling lifelike, especially around the eyes, which seemed to glow with an uncannily human delight.

"Was the silent companion always placed at the top of the stairs?" Bryght asked Alexander Steele, who had followed them into the entryway.

"No. It usually sits by the fire in my study."

"Who moved it?"

Alexander shrugged. "That is a mystery for you to solve, Mr. Bryght. No one seems to know."

"You questioned the servants?"

"Yes, but they all say they were fast asleep, until a cry awakened them."

"Has anything been stolen, Mr. Steele?" asked the constable.

"Not to my knowledge."

"Is there any evidence of a break-in?"

"I have not had time to look. My first concern was for my sister."

"A very natural reaction, if I may say so," said the constable. He then turned to the Runner and said, "Me and my men will look about for signs of a forced entry."

The Runner was not sorry to see them go. It was possible Miss Steele had foiled an attempted burglary, but he doubted that a thief would drag the silent companion up the stairs and risk making a noise. Even for him, the figure was bulky, and as he carried the battered figure up the stairs he knocked it against the steps several times.

After the Runner had placed the painted figure in its approximate position at the top of the stairs and ascertained the location of Mary Steele's bed chamber — it was the room closest to the staircase — he asked that the candles be snuffed so he could better visualize the scene. By this time an early morning light was dimly illuminating the staircase, but he noted it was still possible to be surprised by the painted soldier, whose eyes seemed much less jolly and more sinister in the gloom.

He then asked for the candles to be re-lit and made a careful descent down to the hallway, keeping his eyes on the steps.

"Are you looking for something?" asked Alexander Steele, who had remained at the bottom of the staircase.

"Yes," replied the Runner. "I believe Mr. Carlstone said nothing was moved. But was something removed?"

"Not to my knowledge."

Bryght returned to the drawing room, where he asked Mary Steele, "Do you recall, ma'am, if you lit a candle before you left your bed chamber?"

"I ... I might have done so," she replied.

"But you are not sure?"

"No."

"You were not afraid to wander about the house in the dark?"

"You do not know my sister," said Emily, speaking for the first time. "She is not afraid of anything."

Mary was clearly in a miserable mood, for she acknowledged even this compliment with a dark glance. "I first wished to be sure the sound I had heard was not my imagination. I did not expect to meet anyone at the top of the stairs. A thief would be more likely to try to steal the silver, which is downstairs. If I had heard a noise coming from those rooms, I would have asked Mr. Steele for assistance before I proceeded further."

Theo Bryght silently decided that he pitied any thief who unexpectedly came up against Mary Steele, but he noticed that Alexander Steele seemed pleased to hear himself referred to as a defender of hearth and home. However, it was soon learned that Mr. Steele's services in that capacity would not be needed, at least not that evening.

"No signs of a break-in, Mr. Steele," reported Constable Merriweather. "All the windows and doors are locked and bolted tight. And all the rooms seem to be in order."

"That is a relief," said Alexander Steele. "I suppose."

Ella was returned to her mistress's protection by Theo Bryght, who escorted her to Charlotte's inn. The innkeeper was none too pleased to open the bolted front door in the middle of the night, but once he learned he was standing in the presence of a Bow Street Runner his complaints immediately ceased. Soon there was a small fire warming up one of the private sitting rooms, and a tray laden with cold meats and strong coffee was brought in by a sleepy servant.

While Charlotte and Mrs. Seymour hastily dressed, the Runner insisted Ella have something to eat and drink. When the two ladies did enter, they made a fuss over Ella and would not be calmed until they were certain the servant girl was unharmed.

"I knew something was wrong," said Mrs. Seymour, after she was finally coaxed into sitting down. "Did I not say so, Charlotte?"

"Yes, Auntie," said Charlotte. "Now, Mr. Bryght, let us hear everything that happened."

Theo Bryght gave a brief summary of what he had learned in the Steele home, a retelling that was only interrupted by Mrs. Seymour a few times, as she exclaimed over the dangers of silent companions and too dimly lit staircases. When he was through, the Runner turned to Ella and said, "Can you add anything to this?"

"Shall I start at the beginning of the evening?"

"If you feel it will help us understand what followed."

Ella considered for a moment, before she said, "I am not sure what is important and what is not, because I became ill during supper and my mind was unclear."

"Ill? What happened, Ella?" Charlotte asked with genuine concern.

"That is the problem, my lady, I am not sure. I recall sitting in the kitchen with Cook and Margaret and the others, as we always do. The family had finished eating dinner earlier than usual, since it was only Mr. and Mrs. Steele in the dining room."

"Where were the Miss Steeles?" asked the Runner.

"They were both having a light supper in their rooms."

"At their own request?"

"I believe it was at the suggestion of Mr. Steele. Both of the Miss Steeles had had an upsetting day." Ella stopped, as though she was suddenly recalling something distressing, and then she said, "Is it true Mrs. Watson was found murdered? There were such wild rumors in the kitchen."

"Yes, Ella, what you heard was true. Mrs. Watson was poisoned. It was Mary Steele who discovered the body."

"That explains why Mary was distressed, but why was Emily so upset that she could not go down to the dining room?" asked Charlotte.

"I am not convinced Mary Steele was, indeed, so distressed," commented Bryght. "I could more easily imagine Emily Steele being distressed by the fact that William Halsey was released from prison and yet he neither paid her a visit nor sent a message."

Mrs. Seymour harrumphed her displeasure and said, "That was not how a gentleman behaved in my day."

"I agree, ma'am," said the Runner. "But let us continue with Ella's account of last evening."

"I took a cup of beef broth to Mary Steele, at the request of Mr. Steele. When I asked Emily Steele if I could bring her a tray she insisted she was not hungry. Cook would not hear of her going to bed without eating a bite, and so later I brought up some bread and butter and a pot of chocolate. But Miss Steele did not touch it, except for some of the chocolate. When I brought the tray back down to the kitchen, Cook said it was a shame to waste good food and said those who wished to eat the food could do so. But no one took a thing, on account of the news concerning Mrs. Watson, I think. It awakened their fears about the poisoner, who must still be loose."

"Did Mary Steele drink her beef broth?" asked Bryght.

"I did not see her do it, but the dish was empty when I removed it from her room."

"Did you also refrain from taking anything from Emily Steele's tray?"

"I drank the chocolate, sir. It did seem a shame to throw it out, especially on such a cold night."

"But none of the other servants drank it?"

"No, sir."

"What happened next?"

"We were washing up when I began to feel strange. I was not exactly dizzy, but I began to feel very, very tired. I must have fallen asleep in the kitchen, because the next thing I remember is waking up in the middle of the night, in Margaret's bed chamber."

"Do you think Ella was sedated?" asked Charlotte.

"It is very possible," said Bryght.

"Why would anyone wish to make Ella fall asleep?" asked Mrs. Seymour.

"It is very possible Ella was not the intended victim."

"You think, then, the drug was for Emily Steele?" asked Charlotte.

"If the drug was in the chocolate, then yes, that is exactly what I think." He then asked Ella, "Is it common knowledge that Emily Steele likes chocolate?"

"It is not a drink Mary Steele is fond of," Ella replied. "She prefers tea."

"And I suppose Alexander and Julia Steele prefer coffee," said Charlotte. "I believe that is often drunk on the Continent."

"Yes, my lady," said Ella. "Julia Steele will sometimes take a cup of chocolate with Emily, but she never asks for it for herself."

"And I suppose it is known that whatever is left in the pot, whether it is tea or coffee or chocolate, is drunk by the servants, if they wish?" asked the Runner.

"That is done in most houses," said Charlotte.

"So our 'apothecary' could have accomplished much with just one pot of chocolate. He could have sent Emily Steele and the servants into a deep sleep for most of the night."

"But for what purpose?" asked an exasperated Mrs. Seymour. "To drag a silent companion up an entire flight of steps? It makes no sense."

Theo Bryght asked Ella to continue with her tale, adding that perhaps her account would shed some light on this murky subject. But she could clarify little that he did not already know.

"You did not see the face of the person who was carrying the silent companion up the stairs?" asked Bryght.

"No, he must have been hiding behind the Cavalier."

"You said 'he.' Did you form an impression if it was a man or a woman, perhaps from the lightness or heaviness of the footstep?"

"I did not at the time — and perhaps it was not a man, after all. It could not have been someone very strong, or they would have lifted the silent companion and carried it up the stairs, and not dragged it, to avoid making so much noise."

"Unless they wanted someone to hear them," said Charlotte.

Theo Bryght smiled. "My compliments, my lady. You are beginning to think like a Bow Street Runner."

Charlotte bowed in his direction.

"But why would someone want Ella to hear them?" asked Mrs. Seymour, too engrossed in this puzzle to notice the salute that had passed between her niece and the Runner.

"Not Ella," said Theo Bryght. "The person might have assumed Ella had gone home, as usual, and that the other servants were either sedated or too far away to hear. This performance was most likely done for the benefit of one of the family members, if indeed the person meant for the noise to be heard. However, there is the possibility the noise was unintentional — that, as Ella has suggested, the silent companion was bulkier and heavier than the person had supposed."

"What I cannot understand or explain, sir," said Ella, "is why I did not hear Miss Steele leave her room. I am quite certain I did not hear a door open."

"I would be willing to wager it is for the same reason I did not find a candle or any signs of wax on the stairs or burn marks on the silent companion."

Noting Mrs. Seymour's still puzzled expression, Bryght explained, "One would think Mary Steele would have brought a candle from her bed chamber. But there was no sign of her dropping one in the vicinity of where she fell. And since the silent companion did not go up in flames it is highly unlikely she continued to hold on to the candle while she was falling."

The light of understanding dawned upon Mrs. Seymour's pensive brow. "It was Mary Steele who dragged the silent companion up the stairs!" But then the light dimmed as quickly as it had flared. "Why would she do that?" she wondered aloud. "Who did she wish to startle — and harm? She would not have wished to harm her own sister. And a man cannot be depended upon to be so easily frightened. Therefore, she could not have intended to harm her brother, either. That leaves only

Julia Steele. But why should she wish to injure Mrs. Steele?"

"Your logic is admirable, ma'am, but incomplete." said the Runner. "There is someone you have not yet mentioned."

"Mary Steele?" said Charlotte.

"Yes," said Theo Bryght, "Mary Steele."

Mrs. Seymour shook her head, not at all pleased. "Why go to all the trouble of bringing the silent companion up the stairs? She could have pretended to lose her footing and achieved the same purpose."

"Not quite," replied Theo Bryght. "When an accident occurs there is no one to blame. The presence of the silent companion in an unusual place must suggest to an outsider, such as me or the constable, that someone placed it there to purposely startle someone else. Since Mary Steele's room was closest to the stairs, it was natural she would be the first to be awakened by the sound. Her plan to stage her own near murder would have succeeded, if Ella had not been hiding in the corridor." He then asked Ella, "You are certain the silent companion was not already standing at the top of the stairs when you first heard the noise?"

"I should have noticed it at once, if it was there."

"But who did Mary Steele wish to blame?" asked Mrs. Seymour.

"It seems certain she wished to cast yet more suspicion upon her brother. She did hint he was responsible for poisoning Thomas Steele at the inquest."

"Do you think she is too afraid to accuse him outright of poisoning their father?" asked Charlotte.

"It is awkward when there is only suspicion and no proof," agreed the Runner.

"And he does seem to be lording it over his two sisters, if he is exiling them to their rooms without a decent supper," said Charlotte. "But why, if he knew he would inherit everything, did he not wait until his father died a natural death?"

The Runner's thoughts returned to William Halsey. It was a fault of the age that far too many people accumulated more debt than they would ever be able to repay. Although he did not know how Halsey had accrued his debts — since it did not seem to have a bearing on the events, the Runner had not liked to embarrass the young man by delving more deeply than necessary into his affairs — Bryght could imagine the young Mr. Steele at a gaming table more easily than he could see the young man performing an honest day's work. And the Continent did have its share of gambling houses. But he did not say all that. The subject of gambling debts was yet another topic he did not wish to discuss in the presence of Lady Ashe, for fear it would bring back unpleasant memories of her husband's short life — and untimely death. He therefore said, instead, "Perhaps he could not wait."

The little circle sat in glum silence for several long minutes, each one lost in their own thoughts. Theo Bryght had to admit the events of the night had left him perplexed. Continuing his line of thought, he, unlike the physician, was not convinced that a newcomer to a house could not find a way to slip a draught of poison into a sick person's glass, especially if he was of an impatient nature — or time was of the essence. That line of thought made him think of Lord Lauferby, and he wondered how the young lord's inquiries in London were going. But when he returned his thoughts to Chester, he wondered why, if Mary Steele truly suspected her brother of murdering their father, she had not tried to speak with the Runner about her fears while they were at Mrs. Watson's cottage?

The re-entry of Mrs. Watson into his thoughts broke the spell of his silent reveries. "Did Mr. Steele leave the house during the day?" he asked Ella.

"No, sir. He went to the study after breakfast and remained there, except when he joined Mrs. Steele in the dining room for supper."

"You are sure of that?"

"Yes, sir. He complained several times about the fire not burning properly."

"And the silent companion was by the fire?"

"Yes, sir. I had to move it this way and that, since sometimes Mr. Steele said the fire was too hot and sometimes the room was too drafty."

"It seems almost as though he wished to draw Ella's attention to the thing," said Charlotte.

"That is possible, but if he was in the study all day then he could not have poisoned Mrs. Watson," said the Runner. "And if he did not poison the nurse, most likely he did not murder Thomas Steele. We are therefore still left with the mystery of why Miss Steele is afraid of him."

"Perhaps she is afraid of Mrs. Steele," offered Mrs. Seymour. "I am sure I would not trust a young lady who was raised in Italy."

"Did Mrs. Steele leave the house?" asked the Runner.

"Yes, she went for a drive," said Ella.

"Aha!" exclaimed Mrs. Seymour, in triumph.

"There is no cause for celebration there, Auntie," said Charlotte. "Julia Steele went for a drive with me and

Emily, remember? She remained in the carriage the entire time."

"Murkier and murkier," said the Runner.

They were all silent for several more tense minutes. Then the Runner asked Charlotte if she had succeeded in drawing a portrait of Thomas Steele. Charlotte went to fetch her drawing, and when she returned she also brought the drawings of the three Steele children.

"The likeness between Thomas and Mary Steele is unmistakable," said Charlotte, pointing out the curve of the eyebrows and the chin, as well as the thinness of the lips, on both portraits. "Emily's coloring — her hair and her skin tones — resemble that of Mr. Steele, but her features are much softer. The brother must resemble the mother, because I see only a hint of a resemblance to Thomas Steele."

The Runner nodded his agreement. "Yes, Mary Steele is most definitely her father's daughter. She has the same hardness in her appearance — and the same disposition, I would be willing to wager. But Alexander Steele has strength of will, too, which he may have inherited from his father. Perhaps Emily Steele is strong-willed in her own way, as well. What is certain is that it does not seem to be a happy family. Is that correct, Ella?"

"I would not know, sir," replied the servant, casting her eyes down to the floor.

"You need not worry about being diplomatic," said Charlotte.

"I did enter the family's service after the tragedy, my lady. Perhaps the house would have been a happier one if Mr. Steele had died a natural death."

"I will not press the question," said the Runner. "But tell me this, when the servants were questioned, did you say you were hiding in the corridor the entire time?"

"No, sir. I thought it best not to draw attention to myself."

"Did no one ask how you arrived so quickly? Or why you were dressed for going out at that hour?"

"No, sir."

"Not even Mr. Steele?"

"No. He did not say a word to me. I almost felt as though he did not wish me to speak."

The Runner smiled grimly. "There is a curious game of cat and mouse going on in that house."

"But what is the object of this game, Mr. Bryght?" asked Mrs. Seymour, her brow clouded by a deep puzzlement. "It will not make sense. It will not make sense."

The Runner stared at the older woman. "Mrs. Seymour, ma'am, my compliments. You are a genius!"

CHAPTER XIX
A POCKETFUL OF POISON

THE NEXT MORNING THE RUNNER was in excellent spirits. As often happened when he was working intensely on a crime, his mind had gone to work during his sleep and generously tossed him a solution to yet another aspect of the puzzle upon his awakening. He had to set aside his good spirits, though, for his first visit of the morning: the apothecary on Bridge Street, Mr. Willows, proprietor, from whom he asked for a sleeping draught.

"A sleeping draught in sleepy Chester?" commented Mr. Willows, chuckling softly at his little joke. "Surely our town is not as noisy as London."

"Does no one request a sleeping draught in your fair city?"

Mr. Willows's eyes twinkled benignly from beneath his straggly eyebrows. "Many families rely upon the old remedies, sir; a warm glass of milk before they retire — or something a drop stronger."

"But not all surely, Mr. Willows, or you would not be in business. The Steele family, for instance, they rely upon your services, do they not?"

The apothecary bowed his assent.

"They must have kept you busy these past few days."

"In what way, sir?"

"Did not Mr. Alexander Steele request a sleeping draught yesterday?"

Mr. Willows shook his head.

"I must be mistaken," said the Runner. "But I am on my way to the Steele house now. If anyone in the family requested a draught for Miss Steele, I could take it there for you."

"Miss Steele, sir?"

"Yes, she had a bad fall last night."

"I am very sorry to hear it."

"The family did not ask for anything to help with the pain?"

"No, sir. But some families do like to keep a supply of common remedies on hand. Miss Steele was most particular that her father should have everything he might need, when he needed it, so he should not suffer a moment longer than necessary. She was a most devoted daughter."

"I am sure she was," said the Runner, taking his packet.

After he left the shop, Bryght continued down the Row, in the direction of Number 10 Bridge Street. When he arrived he was surprised to see that Mary Steele was sitting outside, on the Row's balcony, painting. He did notice, though, that she moved her arm stiffly when she lifted the brush to the canvas.

Doffing his hat, he said, "I am happy to see you are feeling better, ma'am."

"I am not feeling better, Mr. Bryght. But I must finish this painting in time for the annual Exhibition. Rose," she added sharply, "hand me that other brush."

Theo Bryght espied the young servant girl, who was sitting on the floor of the balcony amongst the easel and paints. The girl quickly handed up the requested brush.

He then shifted his glance to the busy street below, the scene Miss Steele was painting. He noticed Mr. Tilson was standing in the doorway of the silk mercer's shop.

"I understand that your favorite subject is the Rows, Miss Steele. I wonder you have no interest in the Walls, or the Phoenix Tower."

The paintbrush fell from Mary Steele's hand and rolled down the Row's uneven wooden floor. While Rose scampered after it, the Runner lifted his hat a second time and said, "Good day."

William Halsey stood on the Walls and looked down at the Roodee. The racecourse was empty on that dreary autumn day, mirroring the emptiness he felt inside.

"What is the use, Jack?" he said to his companion.

"It is the principle of the thing," said Mad Jack, who also seemed to be subdued by the inclement weather. "Those stable hands are hiding something from us, Halsey, and I do not like it."

Mad Jack vaulted over the wall, and William Halsey followed him, albeit with less enthusiasm. When they reached the stable, Mad Jack went straight for the stall where The Miller of Dee had been stabled and began to look around, while Halsey watched.

Old Peter had heard the two men enter and he ambled over to the empty stall. "You are looking for something, sir?" he asked, while he tugged at his hat in the direction of Halsey.

"Yes, I am, old man," said Mad Jack. "I am looking for the reason why you hear me every time I enter this place, but you did not hear anyone the night The Miller was killed."

Old Peter pretended to consider the problem. "I have it, sir!" he said after a few moments. "I am awake during the day, which is when you pay your calls."

Mad Jack scowled. "You still insist you neither saw nor heard anyone enter the stable that night?"

"I do, sir. And it is the truth."

"Yet there are those who say they saw Mr. Halsey here."

Old Peter looked at William Halsey. "I do not understand, Mr. Halsey. You know as well as me you were not here."

"But there was someone seen here who was wearing a coat similar to mine."

Old Peter regarded the gentleman's coat with interest. "It is a fine coat, sir, I am sure. But I would not say it was an unusual one. Do not many gentlemen have a coat like it?"

"They do," said Mad Jack impatiently, "which is why the person who was seen here must have been a gentleman—and not you or Sam."

Old Peter looked down at his coat, which was, indeed, a worn garment that had been in fashion a few decades earlier. "Aye, this coat was most likely walking about the streets of Chester before you were born, Mr. Halsey. But for all that, it suits me very well. There is a pocket for my pipe, and one for my tobacco, too, if I had some."

The old man had taken out his pipe while he spoke, and as he did so something fell to the ground. Mad Jack quickly picked up the fallen object and examined it with interest.

"What is this?" he said, as he opened the small white packet and brought a few grains of white powder to his lips. A second later he spat out the powder onto the ground with a violent gesture. "It was you!" he shouted, before he lunged toward Old Peter and grabbed the old man by the throat.

"Have you gone insane?" exclaimed Halsey, trying to free Old Peter from the clutches of his friend.

Meanwhile, Sam, who had heard the ruckus, hurried to the stall and joined the fray. The two of them managed to tear Mad Jack away from the elderly stable hand and barricade him in the empty stall.

"What has gotten into you, Jack?" Halsey demanded.

"The contents of that packet!" Mad Jack pointed to the white packet, which had fallen onto the floor during the scuffle. "It is poison! That old man killed The Miller."

Halsey looked in disbelief from his friend to the old stable hand.

"Taste it, if you do not believe me."

In an instant, both Sam and William Halsey dove for the packet, but Halsey, who was closer, was the quicker of the two.

"He didn't do it!" Sam wailed. "Tell them, Old Peter. Tell them you didn't do it."

Old Peter did not speak. His eyes were fixed upon the packet.

"Well, Old Peter, have you nothing to say?" asked William Halsey.

The old man shook his head, still in a daze. "That is not mine, Mr. Halsey."

"It was in your coat pocket, man," said Mad Jack. "We both saw it fall out."

"My pocket?" Old Peter placed his hands inside the coat's various pockets. "My pocket? My ..." When he removed his hand from an inside pocket, there was another packet sitting in the palm of his hand.

Constable Merriweather did not exactly believe in ghosts, but returning to the scene of a murder did sometimes turn his skin to gooseflesh. He was therefore happy the Bow Street Runner had agreed to accompany him to the cottage of Mrs. Watson.

"You say that the woman — what was her name?" asked the Runner.

"Mrs. Turner," replied the constable.

"You say she came to you this morning?"

"That is correct, Mr. Bryght."

"Did she say why?"

"She said it was preying on her mind."

"You mean she expects a reward, if we do find the money?"

"That thought had occurred to me as well, sir."

"Well," said the Runner, as he glanced around the room, which was furnished as before, as though Mrs. Watson might return at any moment. "I suppose we should begin searching, unless, that is, our good Mrs. Turner happened to mention where the money is hidden."

Constable Merriweather cleared his throat. "She did say it might be worth our while to look closely at the bricks around the hearth. One might be loose."

Theo Bryght laughed. "If the hiding place is so well known, it will be a wonder if the money is still there."

To his surprise, when the loosely fitting brick was discovered, a thick wad of bank notes was found resting in the hiding place.

"Blackmail is a lucrative business," remarked Constable Merriweather, as he counted the loot.

"And a dangerous one," said the Runner. "She did not enjoy the dubious fruits of her labor for long."

He took a last look at the room. Unlike the constable, he had no expectation of meeting the ghost of Mrs. Watson, and so it was not fear he was feeling. Instead, the silent room, with its commonplace furnishings and sordid secrets, made him feel depressed. He had seen so many rooms like it, been privy to so many similar secrets and ignoble lives.

He was about to suggest they leave, when his eye was caught by something that was unusual — a brightly colored coverlet that lay upon the bed. Crafted from pieces of variously patterned silk, its rich and luxurious hues seemed out of place in the otherwise drab room. "That is a pretty piece of work," he remarked to the constable. "I am surprised no one has stepped forward to claim it."

"I told the children of Mrs. Watson to remove nothing until we had finished our investigation. But if you think it will do no harm to take it with us, I know Mrs. Watson's eldest daughter would like to have it. It is a family heirloom of sorts, or so the daughter said."

"By all means take it," said the Runner. "And may it inspire this daughter to take a more beautiful path in life than the one her mother chose."

When the Runner returned to his inn, he was apprised that his presence was requested in the private sitting room at the back.

"He didn't do it!" shouted Sam, jumping up from his chair and running to Bryght before anyone could stop him. "It was me who found the coat and brought it to Old Peter. Put me in jail, Mr. Bryght. I am the guilty one."

"If you prefer the Castle to the stable, I shall see what I can do, Sam. But first I must order my dinner." The Runner looked at the assembled crowd, which included Mad Jack, and asked, "Are you all dining with me? I am not running for office in this fair city, so there is no need to fear I am trying to buy your votes."

"Do not jest with us," growled Mad Jack. "I warn you, I am in a foul mood."

"And I am in a fowl mood. A roasted chicken would suit me admirably," said Bryght, still appraising the motley crowd gathered in the room.

"He is right, Mr. Bryght. This is no jest," said William Halsey. "Jack thinks it was Old Peter who poisoned The Miller of Dee. These packets of poison were found in his pockets."

"But it wasn't Old Peter's coat before this morning," Sam protested. "I got it from one of those old chests in the Phoenix Tower. When Old Peter complained about his back feeling so miserable, because of the rain and cold, I remembered the coat I had seen in that chest, the one where I hid my cap. I didn't think the coat belonged to anyone, honest I didn't."

Bryght examined the packets, being careful to taste only a few grains of the powdery stuff. "Did anyone see you enter the Tower, or take the coat?" he asked Sam.

"No, sir. But if anyone had tried to slug me like they slugged that Lady Runner friend of yours, I would have given them a black eye they would have remembered."

"Lady Runner friend?" remarked Lord Lauferby, bringing his quizzing glass to his eye. That gentleman had returned from London that morning and was sitting in a corner of the room. "What have you been up to, Bryght, while I was away?"

The Runner shot him a silencing glance, and then said to the boy, "Perhaps you are a bruiser, Sam. But if you do not want to go to jail, you must stay away from that Tower until I tell you it is safe to go back there."

"Why are you in such an excellent mood, Bryght?" Lord Lauferby persisted. "Have you found out who killed The Miller of Dee?"

"That is still a mystery. But if these are truly packets of poison, I know who they belong to—and they do not belong to Old Peter."

The old man gave a sigh of relief. "Thank ye, Mr. Bryght, for clearing my name. If I only had a drop of liquor to go with my pipe, my happiness would be complete."

After the others had left, Lord Lauferby joined the Runner at the table, where they awaited the arrival of the first course of their meal.

"You were right about Alexander Steele, Bryght," the young man said. "Although how you suspected the thing I shall never know."

"Do not say that, Lauferby. Stay by my side long enough and you will learn to think like a Bow Street Runner. But what exactly did you find out?"

"Mrs. Amelia Steele, wife of Mr. Thomas Steele, deceased, passed away in Rome in March."

"Cause of death?"

"Fever."

"And the son, Mr. Alexander Steele?"

"Also passed away in March. Same cause."

"Was Alexander Steele married?"

"No. But Amelia Steele had another son, who had a different father. That son was born in Italy, and he is married."

"And he did not die of fever, I presume?"

"According to my source, the other son was very much alive the last time he saw the young man."

"Who was your source for this information, and what was his proof?"

"I cannot name names. Let us just say it was one of our gentlemen sent to Rome by the government to keep an eye on Napoleon's minions. He happened to be dining at my club, and we were introduced. A most fascinating fellow, an excellent talker. Did you know there was an earthquake in Rome last March? Sounds like a terrifying thing to get caught up in. He said he was dining when it happened and a candle that fell from the chandelier nearly set his cravat on fire." Lord Lauferby nervously fingered his own expertly arranged cravat, as though to protect it from a similar danger.

"Fascinating, but what about the Steeles? Did your spy know them well?"

Lauferby looked about the sitting room, to ascertain no one had entered unawares. "Really, Bryght, you do not have to announce to everyone that this gentleman was a spy."

"My apologies to the gentleman, but I doubt anyone in Chester could guess his identity with such sparse information. And I need more proof than a conversation at your club."

"You will take care of this?" said Lauferby, removing a folded newspaper from the pocket of his traveling coat. "It seems the gentleman was rather fond of Mrs. Steele. I promised to return the paper to him."

The Runner quickly glanced through the newspaper, which consisted of only a few pages and was clearly for ladies, since the news items mainly had to do with balls and picnics and teas for the English-speaking community that were in Rome. A short item stuck between an advertisement for a new tooth powder and one claiming a cure for wrinkles and other skin problems described the tragic demise of Mrs. Amelia Steele and her son, Alexander.

"Will it do?" asked Lord Lauferby.

"Yes, it will," replied the Runner, with a smile.

Theo Bryght went to see Mr. Myrditch, the Steele family's solicitor, after his dinner. "It is just one clause of the will I am interested in," he told the solicitor. "The one about what happens to the money if Alexander Steele does not have children at the time of his death."

The solicitor, who was more accustomed to refusing such a request than granting it, gave the Bow Street Runner an icy look. But he removed the will of Thomas Steele from its box and handed it to the Bow Street Runner.

"The two daughters would inherit the bulk of the estate?" asked Bryght, after he had found the relevant clause.

"That is correct," said the solicitor, showing by his terse manner he was answering the Runner's questions only because he had to.

"Did the daughters know about this clause before Mr. Thomas Steele died?"

The solicitor's eyebrows arched upward a small fraction. "What are you implying, sir?"

"I am asking a question, but if you like I will phrase it a different way. Were either of the daughters present when Thomas Steele dictated his instructions?"

Mr. Myrditch's eyebrows inched upward a bit more. "Normally, of course, the heirs would not be present. But after Mr. Steele's second attack of apoplexy, it was difficult to understand him. When he sent for me because he wished to change his will and I saw he was becoming frustrated by my inability to fully understand his wishes, I did ask Miss Mary Steele to come into the room."

"She could understand him?"

"It was remarkable. I attributed her ease to the many hours she must have spent at her father's bedside, attending to his needs."

"What were the changes she overheard?"

"The clause you have inquired about."

"How, exactly, was the will changed?"

"Before, the son inherited the estate absolutely, regardless of whether or not he had any children."

"Did Mr. Steele mention why he wished to change his will?"

Mr. Myrditch frowned. "You are aware of the rather tragic circumstances regarding the marriage of Thomas and Amelia Steele?"

"I am aware that Mrs. Steele took their son, Alexander, with her to Italy when she separated from her husband. I also have heard there was a question concerning the boy's true father."

"It was often on Steele's mind, after he first became ill. The thought that he might be leaving his money, and his business, to another man's son worried him to no end."

"He spoke to you about this worry?"

"Yes, while he was still able to speak. Since there was no way to prove the boy's paternity, one way or the other, I suggested a sort of compromise. Let the good Lord — or fate, if you prefer — decide the matter. If Alexander was truly Thomas Steele's son, let it be proved by grandchildren who would continue the family name. If not, let the fortune revert to the daughters, after Alexander Steele's death."

"The new clause was your suggestion, then?"

"Yes."

"You realized, of course, that the resolution of the question of children might take several years, since children — at least living children — are not always born at once."

"True, and I assumed the young man would have children, whether he was Steele's son or not. I was merely trying to ease the mind of my client, so he could have a peaceful death."

"And it never occurred to you that one, or both, of the daughters might be impatient to see how the issue was resolved?"

"Impatient?"

"Yes, that they might attempt to ensure Alexander Steele died before he had an heir, so they could inherit the money."

"Sir!" the solicitor exclaimed. "You cannot be serious."

The Runner handed back the will. "Actually, I am. Deadly serious."

CHAPTER XX
THE WEIR

EMILY GAZED AT HER VISITOR with a forlorn look that made that visitor inwardly wince.

"It is up to you, Emily," said Charlotte, trying her best not to sound like a disapproving governess. "If you prefer to end it like this, you are perfectly free to do so. But you cannot stay buried in this house, afraid to venture outside in case you should meet Mr. Halsey unexpectedly in the street."

"I should not know what to say."

"There is no need to say much. The important thing is to see him again and to know you can see him again and not fall to pieces."

Emily looked doubtful. "I wish I were more like Mary. She would not cry if Mr. Tilson were to jilt her."

Charlotte started at the mention of Mr. Tilson. Fortunately, Emily was too engrossed in her own troubles to notice. But Charlotte had to get Emily out of the house that afternoon. Theo Bryght was counting on her to succeed. It was her idea to suggest a meeting between Emily Steele and William Halsey, thus accomplishing two things at once.

"You do not need to speak at all, if that is your wish," Charlotte persisted. "We can be strolling down the promenade beside the river. Mr. Halsey and Lord Lauferby can be strolling toward us, from the other direction. We will nod. They will raise their hats. And the agony of the first meeting will be over."

"If I do not have to speak ..."

Charlotte sighed with relief. She was almost convinced, herself, that she was acting totally in Emily's best interests. After all, Chester was a relatively small town in size. The two former lovers were bound to bump into each other sometime. Yes, it was better to orchestrate the meeting when Emily had a friend like Charlotte at her side, since the girl would have nowhere else to turn for sympathy after today, assuming the Runner's plan succeeded.

Theo Bryght sauntered into the silk mercer's shop, as though he had nothing particularly pressing on his mind. Waving away the shop assistants who hurried to offer their services, he instead sought out the store's manager, whom he saluted with a jovial greeting.

"Business is as brisk as ever, I see, Mr. Tilson. But I hope you can spare me a few moments of your valuable time, as a personal favor. I would like your opinion about a coat I am considering buying for a very special person and ..." and as he talked he deftly maneuvered the shop manager to the man's private office.

When they were inside, he shut the door and proceeded to undo the paper that was wrapped around his parcel, all the time keeping up an endless and meaningless prattle.

"It is a very interesting coat, a very interesting fabric, in my inexpert opinion," said the Runner, removing the last of the wrapping. "What do you think?" He held up the coat that Old Peter had been wearing that morning, the one Sam had found in the Phoenix Tower.

Mr. Tilson looked, blanched, and knocked aside the Runner. Theo Bryght pretended to be thrown off balance, and therefore unable to stop the manager from running out the door.

In his panic, Mr. Tilson ran straight to Number 10 Bridge Street, as the Runner had hoped he would. The door was opened to him almost at once by Ella, who had been apprised of the role she was to play.

"I will tell Mr. Steele you are here, sir," she said.

"No! Tell …" Mr. Tilson looked to the top of the staircase. "Mary!" he shouted. "Mary!"

The door to Mary Steele's bed chamber flew open and the lady came to the banister.

"They know!" the shop manager shouted, and then he fled back into the Row.

For a moment he gazed frantically up and down the Row, calculating his chances for escape. He did not know it was a worthless endeavor, since Constable Merriweather had stationed men at all of the staircases that led from the Bridge Street Row down to the street.

Mary Steele grabbed a shawl and a bonnet, as well as a reticule that was stuffed with coins and bank notes. Always practical, she had allowed that this might happen and had planned for it. If she could reach the Black Lion, which served as both alehouse and coaching inn, before the afternoon mail coach departed, she would have ample time to plan her next move. But first she had to reach Northgate Street.

Ella saw only a blur flying down the stairs. Cook, who was immersed in rolling out a pastry crust, thought it must have been one of the servants who rushed into her kitchen, although why the servant was in such a hurry to go down into the storage vault she could not say.

Although Ella was tempted to run after Mary Steele, her orders were to stay in the house. There was no assurance that the desperate woman would not be carrying a pistol or a knife.

And so the woman ran. She knew the Chester vaults like the back of her own hand — which ones tapered off into a dead end of brick wall and which gave on to the next through a small doorway that was almost never locked.

When she thought she heard the sound of menacing voices coming from the street above, she was forced to retrace her steps. But Watergate Street had its Row and underground vaults, as well. She could still reach the Black Lion by taking a more circuitous route, once the vault ended, through the back streets of the town.

The sound of more voices, these even louder than the ones she had heard before, forced her to turn back a second time. And then she wondered at her own stupidity. It was the Eastgate vault she wanted — and from there an almost forgotten passageway that went underneath the Cathedral. And from there she would be practically across the street from the coaching inn. And from there — safety!

In her excitement she brushed against the stone wall and a protrusion in that wall jolted open the clasp of her reticule, sending a handful of coins flying. She knew she would need every sixpence she had, during the long journey that lay ahead of her, and so she hurried after the coins, which were rolling in every direction. It took her only a minute or two to complete the task, and then she once again began to run.

When she reached the furthest end of the vault, she forced herself to remain still so she could slow down her rapidly beating heart and listen. If the constable and his men were not in the area, and so she could safely emerge from her underground hiding place, it was crucial that she maintain her usual calm demeanor. No one must suspect that Mary Steele, Thomas Steele's daughter, had become a fugitive from the law.

Above her, she could hear the sounds of people walking. There was also the occasional murmur of a few passersby. But there were no shouts, no sounds of persons running, no signs that anyone was waiting for her to appear, to entrap her.

She therefore straightened her bonnet and then cautiously ascended a short but steep staircase. She knew what she must do next. There would be a small courtyard which she must traverse. From there she would either proceed straight to the coaching inn or take shelter in an obscure corner of the Cathedral and wait.

But when she reached the street she saw neither courtyard nor Cathedral. To her dismay, she realized she had been running not north, but south. After her attempt to retrieve the fallen coins, she had mistaken the direction. It therefore was not the Black Lion and the mail coach that awaited her, but the River Dee.

Charlotte did not try to engage Emily Steele in conversation as they strolled along the river. It was enough that the girl was there, far away from what must be taking place at Bridge Street at that moment. It was only when she spotted Lord Lauferby and William Halsey in the distance, that she alerted her walking companion to the approaching crisis.

"In another two minutes it will be over," she assured Emily.

To Charlotte's relief, the girl did not begin to cry. Instead, she surprised Charlotte by asking to be told some witty tale. "Let him see me smiling, Lady Ashe. Please."

"With pleasure. Shall I tell you about the first time Ella tried to curl my hair? She was not trained to be a lady's maid, you see, and I was just a Yorkshire girl, really, and so we had to learn about finery and frippery together. Well, the first time she unwrapped the curling papers I knew at once, from the astonished look on her face, something had gone terribly wrong. And when I looked into my looking glass it was my turn to be amazed, for my hair was not just curled — the curls were all sticking out on my head, pointing in every direction, from the ceiling to the four walls. I would have cried, except I was laughing too hard."

Charlotte laughed at the memory and Emily laughed along with her, and it was at that moment that the girl saw, from the corner of her eye, William Halsey. Still smiling, Emily nodded her head in the direction of the young man. He raised his hat, mechanically, and looked as if he wished to speak. But before he could say a word, Emily extended her hand and said, "I understand, Mr. Halsey. It was not meant to be. Let us part as friends. Goodbye."

"Goodbye, Emily. Miss Steele."

William Halsey released her hand, but looked after her, as she and Charlotte continued their stroll along the river. "It has been a long time since I have seen her laugh," he said to Lauferby. "I did love her. I think perhaps I will always love her. If only I were not such a spineless coward, for once, I would—"

A shout stopped him from saying more.

"Stop her! You, there! By the river! Stop her!"

There were only a few people standing by the River Dee on that dreary autumn afternoon and they all stopped and looked about with confusion. The voice that had shouted was a voice of authority, but in the first few moments it was unclear who it was that must be stopped.

Then a furtive figure jumped down onto the embankment and fled in the direction of the river.

"It is Miss Steele!" exclaimed William Halsey.

The two men watched in horror as Mary Steele jumped into the river, straight into the weir, which grasped her to its whirling, wheeling, watery bosom, before thrusting her downward to its drowning bed.

"We must help her," cried out Halsey, frantically trying to remove his great coat.

"Do not be a fool," said Lord Lauferby, trying with equally frantic motions to prevent his friend from approaching the river.

"My life means nothing to me now. Let me at least try to redeem it in this way." He threw off his friend's grasp and dove into the icy river.

Charlotte and Emily had raced to the river's margin by this time, as had Theo Bryght, who had shouted out the first warning command.

"Can you not do something, Mr. Bryght?" Emily pleaded. "Can you not save them?"

"Is there no rope?" the Runner yelled to the few Chester natives who seemed, by their appearance, to have some business on the waterway. "Is there no boat?"

They all stared back at him with blank expressions on their faces, as blank as the surface of the weir, which had devoured its two victims without a trace.

CHAPTER XXI
THE SILK MERCER'S DAUGHTER

CHARLOTTE TOOK EMILY WITH HER to her inn. Although the girl had many questions, it was not the time for answers. First, she needed to recover from her shock.

But after Emily had drunk a glass of port and was tucked into a warm bed, Charlotte retired to her sitting room to wait. She also still had many questions, and she expected Theo Bryght to come to her before the night was over.

First, though, the Runner had other business to attend to. The house at Number 10 Bridge Street had been secured, and so the supposed Mr. and Mrs. Steele were still at home when he called.

Theo Bryght showed the two the newspaper article announcing the deaths of Amelia and Alexander Steele and waited.

"Surely you cannot blame me for trying," said the young man, with an easy laugh as he thrust the newspaper aside. "All my life I heard about the fortune that awaited my half-brother, after his father finally died. I, unfortunately, had no such luck, since my father was an impoverished Italian count who had good looks and pretty ways, but no money in the bank. Therefore, when a letter from England arrived at our apartments in Rome this summer, informing Alexander Steele that his father was dying and wished to see him before that sad event occurred, I thought it a pity to let the opportunity pass by and disappoint the old man. It was really an act of generosity on my part to pretend to be my dead half-brother. Old Thomas Steele got to see his heir, the Miss

Steeles got to see their long-lost brother — it all might have worked out very nicely, if I had been the only one in the family who was unscrupulous and greedy. I never imagined the old man would be poisoned and my dear sister would try to place the blame on me."

"Even a thief needs luck," said the Runner, gathering up the newspaper and sticking it into the inside pocket of his coat, where it would be secure.

"Yes. You can imagine my surprise at the inquest, when I realized I might be hanged for a crime I did not commit. I admit I am a scoundrel, sir, but I am no murderer."

"What do you intend to do with us, Mr. Bryght?" asked Julia, looking more like a china doll, wrapped as she was in her pale silks and furs, than a living woman.

"There is a carriage waiting outside. Get in it and leave Chester at once, without taking any of the Steele fortune with you — not so much as a spoon. If you return to Italy and stay there, I shall do nothing, for the sake of Emily Steele, who has already suffered enough horror and shame. But if you refuse my terms, I shall have the law after you."

"That is very generous of you, sir," said Alexander. "And out of affection for dear Emily, my wife and I shall accept your offer. But we will need time to pack our trunks. We cannot travel without a change of clothes."

"A servant will pack them and send your trunks after you."

The former Mr. and Mrs. Steele accompanied the Runner to the carriage, where an armed escort was already seated inside. After closing the carriage door, Theo Bryght said to the young man, "Remember, do not come back. And do not try to contact Emily Steele, ever. If I do hear that you have appealed to her affectionate nature and tried to con her out of a portion of her fortune, I will hound you to the ends of the earth, sir. I will follow you to hell before I will allow you to deceive that lady again with your sordid tricks."

The Runner gave the signal to the coachman, and the carriage set off. He was not sorry to see it leave.

When he saw Constable Merriweather in the street, the man of law informed him that Mr. Tilson had been safely placed behind bars at the Castle, while a messenger had been sent to Stanley Hall to convey the tragic news of William Halsey's death to his parents.

"And the bodies of Mr. Halsey and Miss Steele?"

"The river will give them up before long, sir. I've posted a few men to keep watch and bring them ashore."

"I suppose, then, we are through."

"There is one more thing, sir," said the constable. "If you wouldn't mind coming with me, I wouldn't mind your being there when I question Mrs. Turner."

"She is waiting to receive her reward?"

"Yes, sir."

Mrs. Turner was, indeed, waiting when the two men arrived at the constable's quarters. She had already heard the news about Mary Steele's death, and after espousing the traditional trite sentiments she ended by saying, "But it was to be expected, after what her father did to some of the folks around here."

Assuming that a longish tale was in the offing, Theo Bryght sat down in the room's most comfortable chair. "Mr. Steele harmed you?"

"Not me, sir. I was speaking about Mrs. Watson."

"Tell us what you know, Mrs. Turner."

The woman did not need further urging. "Mrs. Watson's father was a silk mercer, when he and his missus were first married. He took over his father's business. His shop was on Bridge Street, and there are those of us who still remember it. But he wasn't much of a businessman, it seems, and so when Thomas Steele decided his shop wasn't big enough and he wanted the shop next door as well, he forced Mrs. Watson's father to sell out and at a ridiculously low price. Afterward, her father tried this and that. But nothing turned out for him, and a few years later he died. Some say it was his heart, and some say he took his own life. I only know the widow had no better luck than her husband, and the family went from being comfortably off to being a charity case for the church."

"It's a sad thing when that happens," said the constable, shaking his head sadly from side to side to emphasize his point.

"So it is, constable. So it is," Mrs. Turner agreed. "And Mrs. Watson, being the oldest child and remembering when times had been good, could never forgive Thomas Steele — or the old man's daughters, who walked down the Rows in their fine dresses and with their noses in the air. More than once she said to me, 'Annie, I shall get my revenge. You wait and see.'

"I didn't think much of it when she said it, and even less after she married her Mr. Watson and moved away. But when her husband died and she took up nursing and got herself employed by the Steeles, I said to myself, 'Annie, keep your eyes open, my girl. There is something going on here that may be worth watching.'"

"And was there?" asked the Runner. "Did Mrs. Watson confide in you?"

"She had to tell someone," replied Mrs. Turner with a malevolent twinkle in her eye. "But, mind you, it wasn't murder she was up to."

"What was it then?"

"She only meant to torment the old man—make his life as miserable as he had made her father's life, and hers."

"What exactly did she do?"

"When she saw that Thomas Steele was confined to his bed, and hardly able to move or speak, she came up with the idea of pretending she intended to poison him."

"What?" the constable exclaimed.

"It was all just pretending. When she was stirring his porridge, she would open one of those packets from the apothecary and pretend she was pouring in some poison or other. Then she would watch as he struggled — fighting between fear and hunger and not knowing whether or not to believe her."

"Were the alphabet tiles part of the game?" asked the Runner.

"Oh, yes," replied Mrs. Turner, cheerfully. "She was always a good speller. Like she mentioned at the inquest, her mother forced her to learn how to read and write, so she wouldn't be fooled by the lawyers and the like. She learned how to spell the names of all sorts of poisons. She was very clever, always." Mrs. Turner then drew her chair closer to the Runner. "And that's how she came into her good fortune."

"You are referring to what happened on the day of Mr. Steele's death?"

"Yes, sir. The way she told it to me was that she went down to the kitchen at the usual time for her supper, but the cook had burned something and told her to come back later. Not having anything else to do, she returned to Thomas Steele's room and began to play with the tiles, while talking to him about the nice poison she was going to prepare for him the next day. Well, while she was spelling out the word poison — and she had placed the letter 'P' in the old man's hand, so he could get a good look at what she said she intended to do — she heard the sound of the doorknob turning and she hurried behind a curtain. You see, she wasn't supposed to be in the room at that time, and it wasn't a time for the family to be visiting since they were all supposed to be dressing for dinner, and so she suspected something wasn't right. And that's when she saw it."

"What exactly did she see, Mrs. Turner?"

"She saw Mary Steele take a packet of something out of her work pocket and pour the powder into a glass and fill the glass with some ale that was left in the pitcher and press the glass to her father's lips. When he had drunk it all — and he had no choice but to do what anyone forced him to do — Mary Steele left the room, quiet as a church mouse. A few minutes later, the old man began to get ill, and I can tell you that Mrs. Watson didn't stay to see the end. She ran and hid, until the alarm was sounded and it was safe for her to rush into the room, too."

"And so she tried to blackmail Mary Steele?"

"Not only tried, sir. She succeeded. You found the money she'd hid, didn't you?"

"But she did not succeed for long," commented the constable. "Let that be a lesson to you, Mrs. Turner. You shall have your reward, ma'am, but do not get it into your head to try your hand at blackmail, as well."

"Oh, no, Constable Merriweather," said the woman, shocked to the core. "I'm an honest woman, I am. If poor Mrs. Watson had listened to me, when I told her not to try to get the better of that Mary Steele, she might still be alive today."

The woman, having received her reward for directing the constable to the blackmail money hidden in Mrs. Watson's cottage, was ready to leave, and the Runner had no wish to detain her. But before she left, he asked her one last question.

"This coverlet," he said, pointing to the brightly colored silk quilt, which sat in a corner of the room, "I suppose it was something dear to Mrs. Watson?"

"Yes, indeed, it was," the woman replied, running her hand over the silk squares. "These scraps were all that remained from her father's shop. She said it reminded her of happier times, when she always wore pretty clothes and people pointed to her as she walked down the street, saying, "There goes the silk mercer's daughter.""

"It is certainly not a pretty tale," said Charlotte, after the Runner had repeated the story about Mrs. Watson.

"Tales about greed and envy and revenge seldom are."

Charlotte glanced over at Mrs. Seymour, who was dozing by the fire. In the few days they had been in Chester, this sitting room had become a kind of second home. Although the furnishings were not nearly as grand as the sitting rooms in her Yorkshire home, Hopewell, the comfort of the cushions, the placement of the sofas and the chairs, the cheerful fire casting its warming glow upon the occupants of the room, seemed to invite not only conversation but also a deep appreciation for the things that made life truly worth living — love, esteem, kindness, companionship. More importantly, Charlotte could see herself sitting in such a room for many more evenings to come, happy and contented, if her present companion, Theo Bryght, was seated by her side. She therefore was glad that she and Bryght had this opportunity to speak together freely, with only the dreaming ears of Mrs. Seymour to overhear them.

"It was Mary Steele, then, who killed Mrs. Watson?" she asked.

"Yes. Mr. Tilson may be a shrewd businessman, but he is not a particularly brave person. But since Mary Steele and Mr. Tilson were working together, it hardly matters who did which deed."

"I suppose it did not take much courage to procure the powders and hide them in that coat stashed away in the Phoenix Tower."

"No, Mr. Tilson was a sickly child from youth and continues to suffer from a variety of ailments. So there was nothing suspicious about his frequent trips to the apothecary, or his request for a variety of powders to cure what currently ailed him. He left the packets in the Tower, for Miss Steele to retrieve them at her leisure."

"But it was Mr. Tilson who hit me on the back of the head that day that you and Sam were inside the Tower, was it not?"

"Oh, yes, it was him. Apparently he used to take a walk most days, to get some fresh air and exercise. When he saw Sam and I enter the Tower, he became alarmed. He says he did not wish to cause you actual harm, my lady, but only wished to distract us from whatever it was we were doing in the Tower. He was afraid we would find the coat and the packets of poison that were still stored in the pockets."

"Why did he not just throw the extra packets into the river, after Thomas Steele died?"

"He and Miss Steele did not know when they might need more. In the beginning, they were not sure how they were going to entrap Alexander Steele. They considered the possibility of placing a packet or two on his person — and Mary Steele did drop that packet in the vault, as an attempt to reveal that the poisoner was still in the house. And, of course, having a ready supply of poison came in handy when they wished to put an end to Mrs. Watson and her blackmailing ways."

"Perhaps it is a flaw in my own personality," said Charlotte, "but there is a part of me that feels sorry for Mary Steele. She was her father's devoted servant for all those years. It must have stung her terribly when she found out her father intended to leave her practically nothing, after his death."

"Miss Steele and Mr. Tilson could have married — as was their intention before this sad business began — and started their own business," said the Runner with a shrug. "They were both intelligent and hard-working people, and so there was no reason why they could not have made their own fortune."

Charlotte was not satisfied. As a woman, she knew more about the drudgery of the sickroom than a man ever could. Even when there was great love — as there had been when she helped to care for her dying grandfather — the work was not pleasant. She was certain Mary Steele had gone about her duties in an efficient manner, but she doubted there was much real love between father and daughter. Therefore, the daughter would have expected something in return — some tangible mark of recognition for her devotion in performing the drudgery day after day, week after week. When that recognition did not come, it must have stung the proud woman to the quick, and opened the heretofore wellsprings of resentment and perhaps even hate for a father who demanded all yet gave nothing in return.

"When the opportunity arose — when that new clause was written into the will — it must have been a great temptation."

"Exactly, my lady. It is opportunity that reveals the real person, who they are in their heart."

They were silent for a few minutes. Then Charlotte said, "I am sorry for Emily. She has lost everything."

"Not quite everything. She still has her fortune."

"What good will it do her, now that her love is dead?"

"William Halsey is dead, my lady. But with time let us hope she will have the opportunity to love again."

Charlotte looked away, but she could feel the Runner's eyes upon her. She knew she must come to a decision; in another day, even in another hour, it would be too late. Life had brought them back together for a second chance. This was their moment of opportunity. Most likely there would not be a third one.

"Mr. Bryght," she said, turning back to him, "may I ask a favor?"

"Anything, my lady."

"Please never call me 'my lady' again."

"What, then, shall I call you?" he said, smiling.

She brought her lips close to his and said, "I am sure you will think of something."

CHAPTER XXII
THE MILLER OF DEE

EMILY INSISTED THAT CHARLOTTE and Theo Bryght must marry in Chester, and Charlotte did not have the heart to refuse the girl. Since neither the bride nor the groom belonged to a Chester parish, they did have to apply for a special wedding license, but that seemed a small impediment, when compared with the many losses Emily Steele had so recently incurred. And so the home at Number 10 Bridge Street, which had been the scene of so much tragedy, became a place of joy and excitement as a corps of dressmakers arrived every morning to sew Charlotte's wedding trousseau and Emily busied herself with planning the wedding breakfast and other amusements for the bridal couple.

It also solved the problem of what to do with Miss Steele, who had no chaperon of her own.

Theo Bryght could not remain in Chester the entire time, since his employer at Bow Street was much less sentimental than Miss Steele. But even when he was not physically in Chester, Charlotte knew his thoughts were there. She was confident that her own person was enough to turn his thoughts northward; but at the same time she was not so conceited as to think that she was the only reason why Chester was often on his mind. Even though the mystery of who killed Thomas Steele had been solved, the original puzzle remained just that — a puzzle. Who killed The Miller of Dee?

The fact that William Halsey's life had come to a tragically early end only seemed to make the unsolved mystery even more poignant in the Runner's mind. Not even Mad Jack Mytton's parting words had soothed away the pain.

"You did your best, Bryght," Mytton had said, before leaving the town. "And now Halsey is dead, I suppose it no longer matters."

But it did matter to Theo Bryght. And since it mattered to him, it mattered to Charlotte, as well.

One day she therefore drove to Stanley Hall, with the hope that a woman's interest in the matter — and a woman from their own social milieu — might open doors that remained still shut to Theo Bryght. It was natural for her to express her condolences over the death of William Halsey, and they were graciously accepted by the grieving parents. And Charlotte could not help but notice that this grief was all too real. Sir Richard and Lady Halsey seemed to have aged ten years since she had seen them last.

From there, it was equally natural to express the sentiment, over tea, that she thought it was a pity the mystery of the horse's death had never been solved.

"Why a pity?" asked Lady Halsey.

"Mr. Halsey seemed so interested to know," Charlotte replied. "I should like to see the mystery resolved for his sake, if for no other reason."

When neither Lady Halsey nor Sir Richard replied, other than to offer her more cake, Charlotte decided she must take courage and be more direct. "Sir Richard, I hear you were at the stable that night. Did you see or hear nothing unusual?"

"You have been misinformed, Lady Ashe. I was in Liverpool that night."

"You were seen, Sir Richard."

A look of anger appeared in the man's face. "By whom, Lady Ashe?"

"I believe the man's name was Thaddeus Jones. He owns a tailoring establishment in town, or so I was told."

Lady Halsey gave a cry and grew pale. Sir Richard glared at her, but it took another minute until the color returned to her cheeks.

"Thaddeus Jones is a muddling fool," said Sir Richard.

"He was only trying to help," said Charlotte. "He wanted Mr. Bryght and Mr. Mytton to stop their inquiries concerning the dead horse. He said it would only cause harm, I believe."

"They should have listened to him. You should listen to him, too."

"Then you do know who killed the horse?"

For a moment, Charlotte feared she might be physically and forcibly removed from the drawing room, since Sir Richard had sprung from his seat in an alarming manner. But instead of hurtling her through the closed French window, he began to pace up and down the room.

It was only when his wife joined him, in front of the mantelpiece, and placed a calming hand upon his arm, that Sir Richard was able to regain his composure. "It will come out some time," Lady Halsey said to him, quietly. "The woman is dead. She cannot hurt us now."

Sir Richard nodded, but he did not speak at once. When he did speak, there was a great deal of sadness in his voice.

"I do not know where to begin, Lady Ashe, although the story I am about to tell is a common one, I suppose. When I was a young man I fell in love with a girl from Chester. Her name was Amelia Jones — she was the sister of Thaddeus Jones. I could not marry her, since her father was in trade, and eventually I married Lady

Halsey." He stopped to glance over at his wife. "And I love my wife very much. But ..."

There was an awkward silence until Lady Halsey continued with the tale for him. "Miss Jones was unfortunate in her choice of a husband. She was a pretty girl and one can assume that Thomas Steele was infatuated with her, in the beginning. But their temperaments were not suited to one another. They were not happy together. Is that not so, Sir Richard?"

He nodded, and said, "I sympathized with her plight and, when an opportunity presented itself to us, became her lover. Thomas Steele suspected nothing, at first. Even when Emily was born."

"Emily?" Charlotte gasped.

"Yes, Lady Ashe. Emily Steele is my child, as was the boy Amelia took with her to Italy."

"But then she and William—"

"Were half-brother and sister. That is why I could not allow the marriage between them to take place. I suspect Steele also had an inkling of the truth by then, since Emily does show a resemblance to the Halseys."

Charlotte could not stop herself from staring. In an instant, the trouble of the portraits became clear. The face of Emily Steele had reminded her of someone else — the young man the girl had loved. William Halsey.

"I tried to reason with William," Sir Richard continued. "But he refused to listen. When he threatened to elope with the girl to Gretna Green, if I did not give my consent, I knew I had to take action. I could not tell him the truth, and forever shame my daughter with the badge of illegitimacy, so instead I tried to arrange a feud — something that would make William hate the Steeles.

"That is why I killed The Miller of Dee. I knew the horse meant practically everything to William — that he was counting on The Miller to make his fortune. I bribed Old Peter to keep quiet and drop hints that it was Thomas Steele who was behind the horse's death. I hoped that as the feud escalated either William or Emily would halt their love affair of their own accord. I never dreamed, though, that William would be accused of murdering Thomas Steele, or that he would throw himself into the River Dee. I still do not see why he felt compelled to take his life."

When Charlotte was silent, Sir Richard said, "Now do you understand, Lady Ashe, why it would have been better to leave the mystery unsolved?"

Charlotte shook her head. "Emily is a young girl, and she is alone in the world. She needs a guardian, someone who will look after her, like a father."

"I cannot be that person, Lady Ashe. I cannot bring her into my home. I could not do that to my wife."

"Nonsense, Halsey," said Lady Halsey. "I have no hard feelings towards the girl. Besides, she is a pretty child and she possesses a great fortune. I am sure she will not remain unmarried for long."

If Charlotte could have had her way, the sun would have been shining on her wedding day, bathing the Walls of Chester a brilliant ruddy hue. Instead, the day was grey and damp and dismal — hardly an encouraging start for a new life.

Mrs. Seymour cast several knowing glances toward the window, as though to say, "I told you so." But Charlotte was determined to be happy. Since Theo Bryght was determined to dispel the pervading gloom, as well, while the carriage drove to the church he began to whistle a cheerful tune.

"The melody sounds familiar," said Charlotte. "Does it have words?"

"I am sure it does, if I can remember them," Theo replied. "Let me see …"

He began to sing the song he had heard back in a London alehouse, several weeks earlier:

There was a jolly miller once lived on the river Dee,
He danced and sang from morn till night, no lark so blithe
as he;
And this the burden of his song forever used to be:
'I care for nobody, no not I, if nobody cares for me.
Noooooooooooooo! I care for nobody, if nobody cares for me!'

Charlotte frowned. "The tune is cheerful enough, but I would prefer other words."

"I am at your service, ma'am:

There was a jolly miller once lived on the river Dee,
He danced and sang from morn till night, no lark so blithe
as he;
And this the burden of his song forever used to be:
'I am the happiest man in the world, because you care for
me.
Yeeeeeeeeeeeeeeees! I am the happiest man in the world,
because you care for me!"

ABOUT THE AUTHOR

Jolie Beaumont is the author of *Jericho's Child: A Cozy Regency Romance*, and the Regency mysteries *Ode to a Dead Lord* and *What the Silk Mercer's Daughter Saw*, which feature Bow Street Runner Theo Bryght. She is also the author of the 1930s-era mystery *Set For Murder*.

To find out more about these and future books, visit her website at joliebeaumont.weebly.com.

If you enjoyed this book, please consider telling others about it and leaving a review at your favorite online booksellers. Thank you!

Ode to a Dead Lord
A Theo Bryght, Runner Mystery
"A brilliant story about murder, deception and love" —
Regency Inkwell

It is the summer of 1812. Wellington is fighting Napoleon's army in Spain, Lord Byron is dazzling the Beau Monde with the first Canto of his *Childe Harold's Pilgrimage* – and Viscount Percy Ainsford Foster Ashe is discovered dead in a shabby boarding house in Brighton.

Who would want to murder Viscount Ashe? Is there more to his gambling addiction than meets the eye? Is there any chance that the now penniless widow, Lady Charlotte Ashe, will ever recover her lost fortune? These questions haunt Lady Ashe after she returns to her home in the North York Moors — for as she and Bow Street Runner Theo Bryght soon find out, her husband's death may be just the first canto in a deadly ode to revenge.

Jericho's Child
A Cozy Regency Romance
"A good old fashioned Regency caper" - Romance
Reviews Magazine

Sophie Moore has neither title nor fortune, but she hopes her talent for music will come to her aid, now that she is an orphan and must make her way in the world. But her practical plans take an unexpected turn when she encounters a series of mishaps and misfortunes that lead to a very different future, in the sparkling tradition of a cozy Regency romance.

Set for Murder: A Showbiz Is Murder Mystery
"Charming and suspenseful" – Amazon.com

It's the height of the Depression, but for Penny and Nick Garnett, two young Broadway stars about to make their London debut, life feels like one long musical comedy show — until a duchess is found murdered in her cabin. Who would want to murder the young and beautiful duchess? That's the question Scotland Yard Inspector Guy Travers must solve. When he begins to suspect an over-the-hill vaudeville performer, Penny and Nick rush to help their thespian friend. But with the ship now turned into a "set for murder," will they solve the mystery before the murderer comes back for a second act?